One for Sorrow

One for Sorrow

©Rachel Aisthorpe-19/01/2020

Copyright includes, the cover and everything in between. The characters and plot lines rights are reserved. This prevents individuals from copying any work, distributing copies of it whether free of charge or for sale, renting or lending copies of this book, making an adaptation of this book and making another copy of it for sale or placing the new copy on the internet.

THE CURSE OF EASTMERE SERIES

One for Sorrow

One for Sorrow

One for Sorrow

Dedicated to-
Mrs Glover who ignited the fire
and
Mr Hatfield who fanned the flames into something beautiful.

One for Sorrow

Prologue- 1692

"Witch! Witch! Burn the Witch!" voices tore through the air like jagged blades through flesh.

The caves entrance flashed gold before the girl's wide, terrified eyes. She shielded her emerald eyes from the harsh light with her arm, a cry escaping her lips as she fell backwards on the slick cave floor, jarring her elbow. The scent of smoke travelled down the tunnel towards her like a dark cloud looming over her life, foreboding the upcoming, inevitable, future events. She looked up; fear clenching her chest, her breaths came out it short, sharp pants as she struggled to grasp any oxygen.

"We know you are down there Anna!" a gruff man's voice shouted, eager from the hunt. He spat her name like a curse.

Anna's heart beat as frantically as a mouse's being chased by a cat. Her arm agonisingly ached from where she had fallen as pain laced itself around her. She travelled deeper into the caves in a frantic run, clutching her arm to her chest, tears creating tracks across her dirty cheeks, streaking her muddy skin. Her dress was simple- cut to her ankle with a stained white apron at the waist but it was causing her havoc as it restricted the length of her strides. Her feet bore simple leather boots that were battered from years of use- cool water seeped through the cracks in the leather, making her feet grow cold and numb. Straw-blonde hair was loose in a braid and caressed her face. It was unbrushed, more like a horse's mane then a maiden's hair as it bounced behind her, becoming more free the further and quicker she ran.

      Her family had known about these tunnels ever since they had first settled in what would be called the United States of America. Her grandmother had first started practising the dark arts in the caves and then taught each generation the same art. Anna fled; following the path so familiar to her she did not need light to guide her. She reached a junction and headed straight down the furthest right, until she came to a bend. She followed it, almost instinctually, until she reached the small fire which was surrounded by family heirlooms- old chests, oak chairs, a dining table, a mahogany writing chest and finally an iron cage. The flames of the first torch danced in the draft of the air that tailed Anna as she collapsed into one of the chairs. It was hot in the cavern almost swelteringly so, as she fought to regain her breath. The flames caused shadows to ripple across the stone walls; Anna watched them, mesmerised as if she were a small child. Inside the cavern, Anna felt safe, protected from all sides, despite the chase she was actively in. Frantically, she flicked through the oldest spell book she owned "The Book of Shadows" and arrived at the page she desired. A look crossed her eyes that seemed abnormal, something there was inhuman, it was almost evil.

"Anna!" Adrian called out and Anna felt her whole body soften at the sound of her lovers voice.

She glanced to the entrance where the shadows of the men slowly creeped along the cave wall. Adrian appeared at the entrance, coming to a stop in his tracks when his eyes landed on his wife. The look of worry that was etched onto his features instantly vanished into relief as his eyes met those that belonged to his dear wife. Anna flung herself into him, causing him to stumble back slightly. Tears trickled down her cheeks and soaked into his white shirt as she let the warmth of her husband consume her body. Suddenly, he was torn from her as two gruff hands grasped her shoulders, shaking her roughly. A strangled cry left her lips as she felt her body tense in fear.

"Help me-" a voice groaned from the shadows.

Anna's eyes widened in panic and she started to thrash frantically pleading, "Please no."

"James?" the chief questioned as the man stumbled out of the shadows and rested against the bars, "It is James McCrea, she kidnapped her own brother. She is worse than we thought, witch!"

"No," Anna cried, "You want me, leave him!"

"Listen to her!" Adrian roared as he lunged for the chief but he was restrained back just like his wife.

Anna bled the liquid of her soul as she saw the look of terror that crossed on her husband's face. Hopelessness filled her body as the men began to bash at the bars, using all their strength until they were bent enough for a man to slide through. A sinister smile crawled across James' face, his eyes burning a crimson red deeper than the fires of hell. Before anyone could

realise what had happened, his hands had locked around Adrian's body as his mouth latched onto his neck. Adrian groaned as his eyes rolled back into his head, consciousness was quickly taken from him.
"No!" Anna struggled as more tears flew down her face, "He will kill him."

The mob tried to pry James from Adrian but his lock was like an iron vice, the blacksmith of the town lowered his torch onto James and he cried out, releasing Adrian from his deadly grasp. Anna's captors released her as the men consumed her brother and her husband in flames as they crowded around him. She tried to barge her way through but she couldn't, tears falling quicker and impairing her vision. Adrian stumbled out and into his wife arms, a look of panic consuming his blistering face. It was like an image from hell as Anna stared at her husband's face, nothing but shock clouding her every thought. He collapsed, his body hit the floor with a deafening thud that frightened Anna to the core, his hand on his neck as he tried to stifle the blood flow. Adrian gasped, as if he was trying to release his words and Anna muttered a series of words under her breath.

"We will be together soon," Adrian whispered as he took his final breath, the spell allowing for Anna to hear him. Anna shook her husband violently as she searched for signs of life within him. She muttered every healing spell she could recall only to feel Adrian's body grow cold as she felt life escape him.

Anna cried out, her voice echoing off the damp walls of the caves. She looked towards the towns people for help, for someone to show sympathy but power filled their eyes as the mob continued to torture her brother. They were hungry for more; they were barbarians. Her eyes narrowed into tiny slits as anger invaded her mind and before she knew what she was doing the deed was done.

Her hand grasped a sharp rock and began to carve seven names into the rock, one after the other. In minutes, the cave was covered and she took a glance at the entrance, worry filling her expression. She knew it was nearly over, she had no effort to fight the town off; the battle was over, the war was lost. The sounds of barking hounds was easily recognisable and she knew she was running out of time, reinforcements were coming and James was dead.

"What are you doing Witch?" a gravelly voice demanded, authority laced his voice.

Without a second thought, seven lines were whispered; twenty-eight words burned a hole into the future. Thunder shattered the atmosphere as the cave was filled with a blinding light, radiating from Anna's figure. All eyes fixated on Anna as all attention was diverted to her.

"Give it up Anna, there is no hope for you now witch," a balding man bellowed, grabbing Anna's hand, and shoving her into the iron cage.

Another roar of thunder sounded and Anna released a manic laugh, the evil expression from earlier now invading every feature of her once pure face.

"What have you done?" the air cooled dramatically as he whispered, his voice barely audible. A cool fog rolled into the cave as it suffocated the town, a fog that would suffocate Eastmere for centuries to come and would act as a warning.

From outside the cave, a magpie- black and white against the sky- squawked before flying into the dense forest, swearing that the words Anna whispered, the curse she inflicted, the harm she would bring would never be revealed…

Until Now

Chapter One- Alina

320 years later…

Morning sunlight broke through the small cracks in the pale pink blinds that shielded me from the blinding rays. I could hear the morning chorus being performed by song birds outside, announcing the presence of the rising sun. I stretched my limbs out under the cover, feeling the slumber leave my aching limbs almost immediately. My eye-lids felt heavy as I tried to transition from my dreams into reality. My dog Sunny lay on my feet as she lounged flippantly on my soft bed. Her paws and whiskers twitched as she dreamed; her golden fur the colour of molten light in the rays. I pried my eyes open as I felt my eyelids close, urging me to try and enter slumber once again.

      I rolled over, causing my duvet to rustle and startling Sunny out of her deep sleep. She moved so she was sat on her haunches, gazing at me steadily, if drowsily, and fixing me with her rich brown eyes. Sunny opened her mouth, revealing sharp teeth and a pink tongue. I grinned and reached out a hand for her; she responded and stood up to come closer so I could scratch behind her soft ears. She lay beside me once again as she closed her eyes in appreciation and her tail started to wag excitedly.

"Who's my good girl?" I cooed, to which she replied with sloppy kisses, leaving trails of wet saliva across my face, "No kisses!"

    I giggled which did nothing to seize her attack. I flopped back down into my bed, wishing I could sink into it until I myself was the mattress. Huffing a sigh and forgetting any wishful thinking, I crawled out of the warmth of my bed to drop down onto the pale-creamed coloured stool in front of my vanity table. "I swear hair doesn't do this naturally," I frowned at the lion's mane my dirty blonde hair had been transformed into overnight.

    Sunny came over, clumsily leaping off my bed to weasel her head into my hand for yet another scratch. She sat between my legs, staring up at me with wide, curious eyes. I looked on my vanity for my hairbrush and groaned when I realised it had grown legs and ran away whilst I was asleep.

"Fizzy," I sighed; Sunny whined as if I had forgotten her.

"You hungry girl?" I asked as if expecting her to respond.

    Instead, she trotted to the door and nudged her lead where it hung beside my closed, wooden door. "But it's six in the morning," I shook my head and reached for yesterday's blue jeans and Eastmere high shirt before changing into them, "Come on then."

    I grumbled something about irritating mongrels before heading out into the hallway. Quietly, I pushed the wooden door to my sister's bedroom open, my eyes squinting slightly as my sensitive eyes had to adjust to the change in lighting. The sound of my sister's soft snores was audible as she remained deep in slumber. Her form twisted in her sleep and I found my eyes looking at her sleeping, a small smile tugging at the corners of my lips from the look of joy that she wore on her features. Quickly, I spied my hair brush on her oak bedside table and grabbed it before scurrying back to my room. My hand gently closed the door behind me as I dragged my brush through the tangled mess that was my hair before scrapping it into a high pony tail. Sunny yipped excitedly as I grabbed her lead before padding down the stairs and into the blue tiled kitchen. My parents as well as Fizzy were still in bed, so I grabbed a breakfast bar before walking outside with Sunny in tow after securing her pink lead onto her ruby red collar.

The warm morning air meant I didn't need a jacket but goose bumps still rose along my uncovered arms, tickling them as the fine hairs stood on end. I shivered, I was unsure why however as not even a breeze whisked my hair. Despite the bright sky, a fine cool mist was cast onto the town. The smell of salt water was scented on the air as the ocean boarded the east of the town creating a dull atmosphere. It was pleasantly normal for Eastmere.

Nothing phased Sunny though as she barked ahead of me, trotting ecstatically as she bounded from tree to bush, nose to the ground and bushy tail in the air. I couldn't help but release a giggle, only Sunny could brighten my morning. She led the way down the street, creating the pace as she followed the various scents the town had to offer.

One for Sorrow

Suddenly, I jumped as a bird released a harsh, loud cry. A gust of wind abruptly blew causing for me to shiver and Sunny to whine. The large population of magpies in Eastmere and my exposure to them for some reason had not helped me in evading any unwanted, spooky experiences. My eyes darted around anxiously before a magpie took flight, charging right for me before gliding into the air, stark against the bright blue sky.

"Jesus Christ," I cursed in a slippery tone as my heart hammered against my ribcage violently.

I took a couple of deep breaths to try and calm my heart and breathing back to normal but my body still felt on edge. I glanced at my watch uneasily, knowing I was bridging the gap between night and day a little riskily.

"Are you okay?" an unfamiliar, husky voice questioned.

My body turned to focus on a tall boy who appeared to be of a similar age to me. The first thing I noticed was the bulging box he was carrying and how it showed his rippling muscles. He was clad in a white shirt which was struggling to contain his muscles and jean shorts which he paired with some white converse. The pools of chocolate that were his eyes were hidden beneath strands of fallen, molten brown hair. My eyes found his plump lips which were pulled up at the corners into a friendly smile, my thoughts instantly thinking about how kissable they were.

"Three for a kiss," a menacing voice whispered before it was caught in the slow summer breeze that had seemingly formed.

One for Sorrow

My head whipped around to see who had spoken, knowing for certain that it wasn't the boy as his lips never moved whilst my eyes were fixed on them. Confusion laced itself around my expression at the words that were hidden in the wisps of the wind. I glanced down to Sunny who was cowering, a low whine leaving her shaking form as she laid on her belly in submission. My eyebrows furrowed as confusion invaded all my thoughts, my natural curiosity wondering what was happening. Maybe I was imagining things. He was looking at me as if I was. I had left the house slightly earlier then usual, the remnants of the spooky night was still evident in the air. Something changed at night in Eastmere, the ghosts and ghoulies come out to play. Although nothing has been proven, it's a known fact and Mom and Dad had made Fizzy and I live by it the entirety of our lives.

"You okay?" he questioned again and I nodded, still a bit unsure of myself.

"Thanks for asking," I replied, "Just a bit spooked. This town isn't what it seems to be, you know? See you around anyway, nice to meet you."

"Wait, what do you mean?"

He grabbed my free hand, electric shocks dancing across my skin and I met his chocolaty gaze. Neither of us could move for a second as my jaw slowly crept down. Eastmere never seemed to cease surprising me. Sunny growled at the contact, edging towards me and he dropped my hand, a bashful look crossing his face. I whistled to her to let her know I was fine and she bounded on her longer lead to the next available greenery.

"You'll see," I told him before walking away, Sunny pulling on her lead desperately.

All my life I had been a prisoner to Eastmere. The spooky town had captivated my parents and there was no chance of me moving. Not that I'm sure I wanted to. As strange as it was, it was home. My parents landed in Eastmere twenty years ago when they were a couple of years older than me, touring America until they had to go to college. They vowed after college they would return to Eastmere and they honoured that promise. The two of them set up in our current home and a year later they were married with me on the way. Our family had roots in this town already so my parents said it was something like fate that brought them back to Eastmere. They were always going on about fate and what will happen, will happen. But I prefer to think I control my own fate, not that it's already written for me. Mom and Dad had always implemented the rule of no night walking unless you're in the lit streets with a group of friends. Some of the town were sceptical but Mom particularly was an avid believer that the supernatural element to Eastmere existed.

Another bird cawed and I turned to see what seemed to be hundreds of birds flying my way, charging at the speed of light. As my legs powered me towards the house, my heart hammered in my chest. Nausea filled my body as I took a sharp turn and entered the front garden. I bumped into my sister on the porch, crashing onto the floor in a heap with Sunny stuck between our legs. My chest rose and fell deeply as I caught my breath back, my legs feeling the mile long sprint I had just done and my tail bone aching from the fall. My sister Felicity looked at me credulously through her blonde, wispy fringe before cracking a sheepish grin. Her emerald green eyes stared at me through long lashes as she swiped her blonde hair from her face. She ran her fingers through Sunny's fur before scratching her behind her ears, Sunny panting whilst looking at Fizzy.

"Hey Alina," Fizzy greeted, as she laughed at me, a look of joy crossing over her features, "You're back early."

"Yeah. I got spooked but what else is new in Eastmere. Managed to get to the next row of houses closest to us," I gave a half-hearted smile as I could feel my heart pound in my chest, I hadn't recovered yet, "Met a new boy though."

"A new boy?" Fizzy frowned, it seemed unnatural on her face.

"Yeah, weird I know, haven't seen a new boy since Adrian," I agreed with a laugh, "He seems nice anyway, lives next door to Chad."

"Just nice?" Fizzy laughed, raising an eyebrow in disbelief, "Well I hope he likes music because Chad and Reece seem to get louder each time they practise."

"Shush you," I giggled and Sunny barked at me, "We should probably keep going."

"So, you want me to come with you for protection?" she mocked me with a mischievous glint in her eyes.

One for Sorrow

"I am the older sister, I don't need your protection," I retorted back playfully and Sunny let out a bark of agreement.
"Oh come on then!"

She took one glace to the baby pink mug she had left next to the porch swing, steaming with a fresh cup of tea, but disregarded it like she did my comment before. She placed the book that she was holding when I crashed into her next to the mug, flicking through quickly to place the bookmark back in from where it had fallen. Taking her muddy boots, she pulled them on before jumping to her feet with a sigh.

Her jubilant face lit up in laughter as she grabbed Sunny's lead and skipped out the door, Sunny following behind her blissfully. I shook my head and followed her from the wooden porch and back into the warmth of the morning sun, squinting as my eyes adjusted to the harsh light once again. Cautiously, I took a glance around to reveal that the birds had gone. A sigh of relief escaped my lips and I jogged to catch up to Fizzy, my ponytail tickling the bottom of my neck, causing for my hairs to stand on end once again. For a moment, I paused and wondered whether I had imagined those birds but I knew in my head it wasn't the first time Eastmere had conjured up something weird.

"See nothing to be afraid of," she reassured me with a bright smile, "What did you see anyway?"
"There were hundreds of birds," I explained.
"I don't see anything; I'm sure you imagined it."
"Maybe I did," I shrugged, "Don't you think magpies are creepy though?"

One for Sorrow

"Not really. Shall we take Sunny into the forest?"

Before I could protest, Sunny yipped in agreement and Fizzy headed into the protection of the trees. A nervous gulp travelled the length of my throat but I forced myself to follow anyway.

The sun glistened through the cracks in the trees, the underbrush attempting to soak up what little light came through. Small animals scampered at the sight of Sunny prancing along the dirt trail. Even though everything seemed to be normal, I knew it wasn't. My eyes searched the area, alert, as we walked. I jumped when Fizzy stood on a twig, causing a sharp snapping sound as it crunched beneath her boots. The wind picked up for a moment, whipping my hair in front of my face, blinding me and making me yelp. I felt Sunny's warm presence brush against my legs as she tried to steady me.

"Awe, hello birdy," Fizzy cooed as I brushed my hair from my face frantically.

I did a double take as the magpie cawed, not at Fizzy, at me as it eyed me with pitch black eyes. I felt my body freeze to the spot I was standing in; as it hopped towards me, once, then twice, until it was stood right in front of me and cawed. Beside me, Sunny growled deep in her throat, a sound I would never had associated with her. Fizzy frowned and moved towards Sunny to shush her. Slowly, almost mocking me, the black and white bird spread its midnight wings and began cawing loudly, almost deafeningly before taking to the air and flying through the trees and out of sight.

One for Sorrow

"Are you okay?" Fizzy questioned, placing a comforting hand on my arm, "You seemed freak."
"Did you see that?" I gawped, I could feel my jaw creep down in disbelief.
"Yeah, it was a magpie. It was sweet how it came up to you like that," Fizzy smiled.
"We have two very different opinions about those birds," I shook my head at her.
"Well maybe if you greeted him appropriately then you might not feel the bad omen," Fizzy teased.
"What? Hello Mr Magpie, how's your wife? That's going to solve all of my problems?" I shook my head.

Sunny gave her a disapproving look, as if she understood Fizzy as she bumped against my legs again. I knew Eastmere was a strange town as far as normal goes in today's society but this was strangest I had ever seen it. I didn't know what was going on and I couldn't believe Fizzy was playing it off as being normal. Mom and Dad had always warned us that night was different in the town, something to do with where the town rested but I just shrugged it off to Mom's superstitions.

"Come on, look. Sunny is getting bored," I motioned towards my golden retriever who had taken interest in a small pine sampling.
"You weren't scared, were you?" Fizzy teased, grinning as joy lit up her face.
"Of course not," I replied, shrugging her off as she wrapped her surprisingly strong tanned arms around my waist.

Fizzy danced away from me as I moved to pull her hair, laughing manically as she did. I whistled to

Sunny who came trotting over, looking pleased with herself, before bending down to her level.
"Sunny, attack!" I exclaimed pointing at Fizzy.
"Oh no!" Fizzy looked mock-horrified before running down the trail, a golden ball of fur chasing after her, barking.

I laughed, a smile chasing away any memory of the strange bird.
"Argh!" Fizzy cried as Sunny caught up to her and knocked her over, pinning Fizzy to the ground and smothering her in sloppy kisses, "No kisses, I surrender!"

She giggled, pushing Sunny away from her and I laughed, almost uncontrollably as Sunny continued her attack. A golden tail wagged back and forth as excitement filled her small form.
"Come on, girl. Sunny!" I called to her, patting my hip between hiccups of laughs as I tried to summon her back to me.

Sunny bounded towards me and found a very interesting bush. I helped Fizzy to her feet and brushed dead leaves and debris from her clothes and hair.
"Thanks," Fizzy gave me a pointed look and shoved me away.

Both of us laughed before racing back to our house through the forest. We both paused at the door panting for breath as I unclipped Sunny's lead and she bounded into the house.
"You looking forward to the first day of school tomorrow?" Fizzy asked.
 "Of course, it'll be nice to see everyone," I nodded my head, "Last Sunday to chill though."

One for Sorrow

"Speak for yourself, I'm trying to get this violin piece mastered ready for auditions, feel as if I've got a shot this year," Fizzy grinned.
"You're talented Fiz, you should have more confidence in yourself," I smiled and she just squeezed me thankfully.

Mom and Dad were still in bed so I headed to the kitchen whilst Fizzy went to the shower to freshen up. As I entered the kitchen, my stomach growled, it was definitely time for some more food. My hand grasped the cool metal of the fridge as I pulled it open, staring at its contents blankly for a couple of seconds before grabbing a few different items for breakfast.
"Morning honey," Dad greeted, I smiled to him as I cracked two eggs into the bowl.

Before I knew it, I had Sunny at the bottom of my feet, begging for the sausage I was holding which I was about to throw into the frying pan. A small laugh escaped my lips as I threw her some fat from the bacon onto the floor.
"Do you fancy making breakfast for your lovely family?" My mom came up beside me, grasping the top of my arms playfully with a pleading look on her face, batting her eyelashes at me. I gave a heaving sigh before nodding, a teasing smirk plastered on my lips.

Mom hummed like the morning birds as she waited for the coffee to brew, absent-mindedly drumming the spoon against the palm of her hand. Dad shook his head at her as he sat at the breakfast bar, glancing over yesterday's newspaper as he did so. A loud scream penetrated the atmosphere in the house, causing us all to stop in our tracks. I dropped what I

was holding, the metal tongs clattering to the floor deafeningly so and darted up the stairs, taking them two by two and almost falling on the way. Sunny jumped at the door as we approached it, demanding entry. Pushing the bathroom door open, my gaze met Fizzy who was instantly filled with relief. She clutched the cream towel to her tightly, her hair falling across her face and impairing her vision slightly. Pointing with her finger, she motioned towards a small spider that scurried into the smallest crack between the ivory tiles. Sunny seemingly knew how pathetic Fizzy was being as she turned, tail in the air as if she was disgusted and trotted downstairs. I tried not to laugh at Sunny as she disappeared from sight.
"There was a spider," she smiled innocently and I shook my head at her with a laugh.
"Who's scared now?"
"It caught me by surprise," she huffed, pulling the shower door to a close.

    I said nothing to her but just allowed the smirk to naturally form on my face as she threw a towel at me, Mom shaking her head at her two daughters. Fizzy gave a playful grin before pushing the door to a close, the sound echoing across the hallway.
"Sisters," I laughed as I bounded down the stairs, finding Sunny licking at the tongs I was using to put the bacon onto the grill.

    I tutted to her as she turned to me, what seemingly could be a grin plastered on her doggy face. A smile formed on my lips as I continued to make breakfast peacefully.

Chapter Two- Alina

"Ah Alina, great timing. Could you show Damon to his next lesson please? We've timetabled him to be in all of your lessons," the principle smiled politely at me and I nodded, "This is Alina Harrington, she's one of our spokespeople for the school and head cheerleader of the junior team."

"Hi," Damon shot me a bright smile, something familiar flicking into my mind and it was then that I remembered his face. My heart fluttered slightly as I remembered our encounter from yesterday. I touched my left hand as I remembered the sparks that had rushed up my arm at his contact. Evidently, by the huge grin that was pulling at his lips from ear to ear, he remembered me too.

"Hey," I greeted, giving him a small wave of my hand.

"Well, I will leave you two to it, have a nice day," the principle gave a polite nod of his head and I fluttered my fingers as a way of bidding goodbye to him.

Damon and I turned in the opposite direction to the head teacher and began walking the emptying corridors of Eastmere High.

"Not spooked anymore?" he laughed and I shook my head, a fluster of red hitting my cheeks.

"No," I mumbled, gesturing for him to walk through the open door before I did.

"Alina's a pretty name," Damon commented, I was struggling to tell whether he was flirting with me or just giving me an observation.
"It's meaning isn't so pretty," I shrugged, dismissing his comment but when he turned to me with a curious look on his face I continued, "It means "alone" in Dutch."
"Oh," Damon frowned, almost as if he was feeling sorry for me.

We took a few steps forward, slowly as if both of us wanted to stay in each other's company for a few moments. I found myself searching for a topic of conversation but Damon stopped and turned towards me before I could come up with an idea. I found myself wanting to stare at him, try to figure out his type of character but I quickly realised he wasn't an open book.
"So, what's it like here at Eastmere High?" he questioned, setting off again as he followed my route.
"It's just your regular high school, this is a good shortcut to get to the science block by the way," I answered honestly and he laughed, "Why did you move here?"
"Dad's job," he admitted with an exasperated sigh, boredom was laced into his expression, "That's what the usual reason is, though he promised this would be the last time before I graduate so I guess that's something."
I nodded in understanding, "Did you move in yesterday or?"
"No Saturday, there was only a few boxes left and wanted to get them sorted early on so I could chill

One for Sorrow

Sunday afternoon before school kicked off," he responded.

We walked across the football pitch towards the science block, the cool breeze nipping at my skin viciously. Damon gazed out across the deserted field, an absent look crossed his features. He didn't stop walking however so I just kept up with his pace.
"Can't wait for basketball season to kick off," Damon grinned.
"Ah, you're a basketball player?" I asked.
"Yeah, football was never really my thing to be honest," he admitted.
Before I could respond to his question, Alexa, my cousin, bounded into my sight. Her face changed from a scowl to neutral expression, guess that's the most I could expect from her, "Is cheer on later?"
"Yep, all teams," I confirmed before a male admirer rushed her away, his arm snaking around her waist until she was drawn into him as they walked. Her rich brown hair swayed in time with her short skater skirt, typical Alexa.
"She was definitely something," Damon commented, I knew what he was referring to almost immediately, it was what the whole school referred to.
"She's my friend," I shot him a look and his eyes widened.
"I… I'm sorry…"

I cut him off by laughing. Watching him shake his head with an amused grin on his face was priceless. I bent over in laughter as I tried to sober up, he just remained silent as he waited for me to control my laughter. The sheepish look that was appearing on his face urged me to stop laughing and explain myself, I didn't want him to hate me or for me to embarrass him too much.

"I don't know if we're friends as such. We're cousins, and she's sort of in our group, but, I must admit, she is an acquired taste. She's always snapping at me about how she would make a better head cheerleader. She wouldn't be head though, she's a senior so she's not on our team," Damon gave me a questioning glance and I sighed before turning to him again, "Yeah, I'm babbling, aren't I?"

"It's cute," he commented, making me giggle and my heart skip a beat.

"Anyway, first class is chemistry with the world's most boring teacher. He's wider than he is tall and has a voice that will make you want to fall asleep. Just make sure you take notes though or mister boring becomes mister messyourpantsscary. If anyone asks, I didn't say that, I'm supposed to have a positive opinion of all the staff here at Eastmere High," there was a fake enthusiasm in my voice that Damon caught on quickly to.

    Damon laughed, he had a rich warm laugh, the kind of laugh that made me want to laugh along with him. It reminded me of his eyes, it had the silkiness of melted chocolate in the tone of it. I could feel myself getting lost in my thoughts as Damon paused to look at me with a spark of curiosity in his eyes. My head bowed forward enough for my thick hair to shroud my face, allowing for him to be oblivious to the blush creeping on my cheeks until it had disappeared back to my normal pale skin.

"And due to it being history last, we'll have the task of doing an essay on the history of Eastmere. Actually, you're unlucky enough to have joined the school in time for the briefing lesson," I explained.

Damon's face changed into one of mock horror. I hit his arm playfully, laughing as he dodged me, a grin on his face. I paused for a moment as we arrived into the science block. His eyes found mine as he questioned my lack of movement. Quickly, I was drowning in the depths of his eyes with no chance of escaping when the shrill sound of the school bell suddenly shocked me out of my stupor.

"You can walk with us if you want, around the town, it'll be quicker," I offered as I remembered where the conversation was and he accepted with a nod and a smile, "I'm having a small get together at the weekend, a pool party and I think it would be good if you came, to get to know some people. There won't be a huge amount of people there but enough for you to make some acquaintances and stuff," my words became drawn out as I realised that I was rambling again. I felt warmth hit my cheeks but Damon was still looking at me as if I had done nothing wrong. I tried to swallow the huge lump that was forming in my throat so I could carry on the conversation.

"What's the occasion?" He enquired.

"End of summer, just a celebration to reminisce about the summer we had," I explained, "It's just a bit of an excuse to use the pool before it gets too cold really."

"I'll think about it." He smirked, a playful tone in his voice.

One for Sorrow

We continued to make our way down the now emptying corridors, the odd person running by and greeting me politely. My eyes noticed the look of amazement that was slowly spreading across Damon's features but failed to question why it was there. Just before I was about to enter the lab, he grabbed my wrist similarly to how he did yesterday. My mind flashed back to the day before and I felt blood rush to my cheeks again.
"So, you're nice to everyone?" he questioned and I nodded with a frown.
"Why?" I asked with a laugh.
My eyes glanced into the classroom to see the class settled but I failed to care about my perfect attendance, I wanted to be with Damon.
"You're not a stereotypical cheerleader, are you?" I shook my head brashly at him.
"Of course not!" I shrieked, taking my arm from his grasp, offended, "Do I look like a slutty, snarky cheerleader?"
"You look like a hot, beautiful cheerleader to me," Damon replied with a smirk but I brushed his words away.
"This is the chemistry lab," I announced, "Just don't sit too near the front," I warned, moving past him to get into the class.
"Wait," he said, grabbing my wrist again, my body reacting similarly to how it had yesterday. I hated that my body betrayed me instantly. He pleaded with his light brown eyes adorably and I found my heart melting, "I'm sorry."

"Apology accepted," I replied, before walking to take a seat next to my best friend, Bridget. I wondered how many times my body would respond to him like that as I took my seat, tingles were slowly fading from my wrist where his fingers had grasped it. Bridget just glanced at me with an incredulous look on her face.

Bridget noticed almost immediately that my conversation with Damon wasn't normal and as always was particularly observational towards me. She wore her long black hair to her waist, her heart-shaped face looking at me curiously with a pallor held in it. She wore a plain black skater dress to the knee showing her athletic yet feminine figure thanks to her being a cheerleader for the past year. There was no question that Bridget wasn't beautiful and she had a kind heart yet guys didn't seem to surround her. The only thing that made her unusual was her eyes, they were stunning. They were this rich almost navy blue, so deep in colour it felt as if you were swimming in the deepest ocean trench. The pupil wasn't visible as if it had drowned in the deep colour. In the light, they appeared almost purple.

"Who's he?" she hissed a whisper at me as Damon frowned at the teacher, trying to take in what he said. "New boy, clueless about the anomaly that is Eastmere. He's coming to do our assignment after school with us," I explained and she nodded before taking a quick look at him.

I watched as her violet eyes scanned over him before a smirk fell onto her lips. Bridget understood me completely, that was my favourite thing about our relationship.

One for Sorrow

"Now Class, please welcome a new student, Damon," everyone's eyes turned to him and Damon shrunk in his seat two rows from the front. I could see the red creeping up his neck and onto his cheeks and the familiar look of wanting the ground to open up until it would swallow him and his wooden lab desk whole. "Well done sir," I muttered as disappointment crossed my mind, "Well done."

Bridget released a long sigh as she thought the same thing as I had, we just glanced to each other with knowing looks on our faces.

"So, he's a definite ten, huh?" Bridget grinned at me over her chicken salad sandwich.
"He is cute," I admitted, feeling my cheeks redden as blood rushed to my head.

I tried to hide it behind my thick blonde hair as I tucked into my own delicious lunch. Quickly, I tried to fill my mouth with as much food as I could before it would look weird to try and avoid anymore of her questions. The school cafeteria was as loud and as boisterous as ever. The disappointment of the new year of school setting in for all the students and the desperation for the summer gossip hung thick in the air. Trays clattered and the sound of bags being slung under the tables was audible everywhere. Just another typical lunch period at Eastmere High. I sat at our usual table with Bridget as we had just finished our gym period that we had together.

One for Sorrow

"Well, don't look now but tall, dark and handsome just walked in," Bridget smirked, her eyes twinkling with mischief.

I turned, a frown on my lips in confusion, until I saw who Bridget was talking about. The last new kid to enter the halls of the school, Adrian Morris had just walked in. He was hot, but not to my taste, though I could tell Bridget was interested ever since he showed up last fall. For some reason, there was just something about him I couldn't put my finger on what allowed me to see him as a friend and not a love interest. I shook that feeling though as soon as I could tell that Bridget had her eyes on him. Alexa hadn't however, for whom it appeared was her personal goal to sleep with the entire male population of the school. I didn't question that though. I just let her be who she was. Many girls in the school had a crush on Adrian but he wasn't interested in any of them, the only girl he really talked to on a deep level was Bridget; it had always been that way.

"Hello, are you doing your history assignment after school?" he enquired, taking the seat next to me and dumping his bag between the two of us.

"Yeah, it makes sense to go with our teacher, that way we can get all the information from him, makes essay writing a lot easier. The whole group is going as well, and I invited the new boy," I stated.

"At last, some new re-enforcements," he cheered though a look of sorrow was still etched into his features ironically.

"Re-enforcements?" Alexa asked, her voice husky as she sauntered towards us and slid smoothly into place next to Adrian.

Adrian ignored her and carried on talking to Bridget which was something the whole table noticed. She had been explaining that we met him in chemistry, which Adrian missed this morning. He mumbled something about a doctor's appointment to which Bridget asked if he was all right. He gave a sharp nod of his head to confirm his health. I had the feeling that they were talking about a hidden conversation but I shook the feeling, it was none of my business anyway.
"Another boy," he clarified after a while and Bridget smiled, her almost purple eyes glittering.
"Speaking of which," Alexa muttered as her current boyfriend- I think he was called Harrison- sank down next to Alexa.
"Hello babe," Harrison said putting a casual arm across her shoulders.
"Harry…" Alexa drawled, giving Harrison a look I could only describe as saucy, but pitying, "This has been fun and all, but it's been almost a month now, and I'm bored."
"Alexa, I-"Harrison tried moving his arm from her shoulders to clutch one of her tanned, manicured hands, "I can change, we could-"
"No Harry," Alexa looked down before making eye contact with him again, "It's over."

Adrian released a chuckle, his face unmoving from his emotionless expression and with a shake of his head, he took his bag and left the table. Alexa watched him curiously, an almost inquisitive look on her features.

"Are you breaking up with me?" Harrison choked out, Alexa turning her attention to the heartbroken boy.

"It was fun. I'll see you around Harry."

Alexa had literally just dismissed him. Harrison's face fell as I watched him slowly stand up and walk away.

"That must be a new record Alexa," Bridget grinned, if a little meanly, "A whole three weeks and two days? Surely, not even one affair."

"At least I can actually get a boyfriend," Alexa sneered back.

Bridget did all the quick, snarky comments for our little duo, but it did allow me to avoid drama at family events. Bridget pulled a face back that earned a disapproving grumble from Alexa. Alexa muttered something about men and smug freaking bitches before unwrapping a chicken tikka wrap.

"At least I haven't slept with Mr Ford," Bridget giggled into my ear; earning me to almost spit my lunch all over her.

Alexa glared as if she had heard Bridget. I knew that was just a rumour, but it was kind of funny to see Alexa's face when she heard people talking about it.

"Are you all still good for coming over at the weekend?" I questioned, Alexa just nodded absent-mindedly and Bridget mumbled a confirmation, "What about Adrian?"

We both remained silent for a couple of seconds as Alexa grabbed her bag and strutted away,

seemingly fuming. Bridget shot me a look which could only suggest she took it too far but I shrugged it off, Alexa had heard worse.
"Adrian?" I redirected the conversation back to where we were.
"I think he said he was good for it. He said we could walk together since we live near each other," Bridget replied, "Are you inviting Damon?"
"That's good, I have done yeah, it would be good if he got to know some of the people in the school and stuff," I tried to reason an excuse for my invitation to him, not just because I wanted to spend time with him.
"Sure," Bridget laughed as she bit into her apple.
I felt blood rush to my cheeks for the second time during my lunch period. I used the same tactic as earlier and tried to fill my face with my fruit salad. Damon's face suddenly became visible to me in a sea of faces. My heart fluttered slightly as I waved him over. He sat down next to me on the end and just gave a polite nod towards Bridget.
"This is Bridget," I introduced.
"Hi," he grinned, "I was just coming back from the guidance counsellor's office, usual chat about how you're fitting in. Anyway, I'm sure I got lost on the way back and I heard the most phenomenal violin piece. I couldn't see who was playing it but wow."
"That's my sister Fizzy," I grinned at him proudly, "Do you play?"
"Piano, a bit, but I'm mostly self-taught," he admitted.
    Before I could get another word in, Fizzy showed up a few minutes later with her lunch. Her face

was flushed as she had been running, her soft blonde curls all over her face, shrouding her.

"Did Alexa dump Harrison then?" she asked Bridget who nodded so Fizzy held out her hand, "You owe me two dollars then?"

"You owe me two dollars I believe," Bridget smirked.

"Dam," Fizzy groaned before digging out two green notes and handing them over as she realised she had lost out.

"A pleasure doing business with you, ma'am," Bridget smiled, placing the dollars with intended slowness into her baby blue purse, simpering as she did.

"I bet you five dollars she's going out with Ian before the end of the week," Fizzy shot back, holding out an expectant hand.

I rolled my eyes at her rash decision, but at least it wasn't as rash as her last bet. Fizzy was always up for a laugh and her and Bridget's bets always provided a good one. Though Fizzy was the one who usually lost out, she wasn't very lucky when it came to betting.

"Done, though I think she has her eyes on Andy Fisher."

"Andy Fisher, yeah right."

"I don't know, she did say he was cute. Plus, he gave her a valentine's card," I put in.

"As did the majority of the male population in the school," Bridget shrugged.

"Whatever," Fizzy brushed her manic hair from her face and pointed across the canteen, "I'd keep your money away from your mouth and into my purse if I were you."

Bridget and I looked over to where Fizzy pointed to see Alexa seating herself next Ian. "We'll see," Bridget replied, taking a sudden interest in her food.

I grinned at Fizzy, before turning to my food as Bridget did. Damon just looked between the group slightly gobsmacked and I smirked, he'd have to get used to it if he was going to fit in around here.

Chapter Three- Adrian

I was stood under the stone statue in the middle of the town, checking my watch when Alexa strode up to me, a sultry smile on her face. I will admit she was a beautiful girl, everything I knew to be desirable to the male species, even for her kind, but she was not my type. For one thing, her smell was off-putting for my senses and made my inner monster rage.

Rain drizzled down in a grey sheet, obscuring even my vision. Clouds had rolled over Eastmere mid-afternoon and seemed to engulf the blue sky. A light mist had cocooned the town, the air cooling dramatically from what we had experienced over the summer. It was meant to be cold, but I did not feel it, even in just my thin shirt and jacket. If I could I would have shivered though to make me feel alive. Leaning against this statue brought back memories I did not want to remember, no matter how much I needed to recall them. Alexa huffed at my silence and began preening her glossy hair when I did not acknowledge her, re-applying red lip gloss to her already scarlet lips. I knew I was being rude but I did not know how else to get the message across to her, I was not interested in anything from her.

I had known her family for years, had known her great, great grandmother, she was one of mine and

One for Sorrow

Anna's descendent, as was Alina. Ironically, she was the mirror image of her, except for the elaborate hair style and different clothes. I think she looked better in the old-style dresses rather than the tight blue blouse and mid-thigh length pencil skirt. The hood of her pale green designer coat hid her face, as she attempted to keep her hair protected from the cold drizzle of the rain. Sometimes I wondered why I did not feel closer to Alexa, Alina and Fizzy since we were family but I just did not. My best presumption was that I had accepted my loneliness long before they came along and opening up to them would complicate me and my miserable life. As darkness had fallen on the town, the nightly critters chattered in the bushes, much less harmful then the dangers that lurked in the forest.
"So, are you doing anything tomorrow night?" Alexa asked, looking up from the screen of her own phone.
"Studying most likely," I replied simply to her through my lying lips.
"Need help with that?" she continued the conversation as she noticed my attempt to unlock my phone.

    As the breeze blew through the town centre, a musky scent was caught on the wind. I felt my monster anger instantly, he was raging, he was breaking free. My fangs nearly impaled my lower lip until a calming aura filled the air.
"Hi guys," Bridget greeted as she jogged towards us, her black curls bouncing behind her. A strange glow emitted from her form as the small amount of skin she let show seemed iridescent. She gave me a questioning smile.
"Hello," I greeted with a forced smile on my lips.

One for Sorrow

Alexa seemingly rolled her eyes, a usual greeting she used when in converse with Bridget. I failed to understand why Alexa disliked Bridget as much as she did but the ways of Alexa's kind were always something I had failed to comprehend.
"How was your first day back?" Bridget questioned, standing beside me until our shoulders were almost touching. I was completely aware of her proximity, so much so that her scent clouded my thoughts.

Before I could get another word in, Alina and Damon showed up, smiles filling both of their faces as they shared a private conversation and the rest of the class followed shortly afterwards, almost as if they had come from the same place. Fizzy was last to arrive, despite her perfect attendance, she almost always seemed to be late to everything. Our history teacher, Mr Geoffries was with the group. The man was recently married actually, not surprising when you considered his good looks and youth.
"Hello," I greeted my group of friends, the ghost of a smile flickered across my face. Bridget just look up at me and smiled.

I knew what she was too, and I hated to admit it, but if my heart still beat she would make my heart beat like a jack rabbit. She was just so radiant, like a beacon in the dark. Her kind was known to stand against the others, but she glowed like a morning star, radiating her love and warmth. It was ironic, considering her kind, but yet there was something pure to her being and existence. Alexa huffed again next to me and moved away to grab a new victim, probably keep him in her clutches for a short while, before breaking their heart. I knew Alexa was not interested in me, her kind and my kind just did not court with one another. But I could not comprehend why she persisted on grasping onto me so tightly. I was sure she could sense my inner monster as I had hers but sometimes, I was unsure due to her lingering.

"Do you want to be in our group? We were going to check out the cliffs, see if we can find the witches cave," Alina explained coming up to her friends and glancing between Bridget and me.

"Yes," I agreed.

Alina handed me a clipboard with a bright smile before turning to Damon.

"Do you know any of the background of Eastmere?" Bridget asked her almost-purple eyes wide and shiny.

I preferred not to think about the past of Eastmere, when I was nothing more than an average seventeen-year-old trying to make a life for myself in Eastmere, just as my parents had. They had owned a furniture store on the main street and lived in the rooms above the store. Father had taught me to be a carpenter just as how he had been. It had been small, but not cramped, and it had been comfortable and ultimately my home. I did not remember much, could not remember friends or family; my parent's image was vague. I had a feeling we had a dog too but that was it, that was all I could remember. Eastmere was not like it is today in the sense of the town's atmosphere, the curse changed something that night. The fog rolled in until it seemingly suffocated everything good within the town and left nothing but a devastating curse with an unknown purpose.

One for Sorrow

The only clear image of my human life was the witch trials, the day they burned Anna McCrea at the stake, and the whole town's aura changed. But I preferred not to dwell on that. It belonged in the past and the whole ordeal meant nothing to me anymore. I just wanted to know what my wife did all of them years ago and whether it was true. I could not comprehend the woman I loved doing something like that, but even I had to admit, that there were many things in Eastmere that did not add up.

"You can't go there!" Mr Geoffries suddenly cut it, "It's just a rumour and even if it is true, all caves on the cliffs have been announced dangerous."

"What's dangerous about that?" Alexa sighed, not taking her eye from the mirror as she applied another layer of lipstick.

"The dangerous part," Bridget answered for the teacher and we all burst into fits of laughter.

Alexa huffed before crossing her arms over her chest dramatically. Her eyes rolled so far back into her head I wondered whether they would return to their normal position. I knew what she meant however, it was dangerous for a human to go into the cliff's but for people like us, probably not.

"Just leave it guys," Felicity spoke for the first time, "We're not sure if it's true so it is not part of the town's history, we shouldn't have even spoken about the cliffs."

A rush of wind rustled the surrounding trees and we all looked around. Alexa's eyes flashed yellow suddenly and her eyes narrowed onto mine, there was no debating whether she knew what I was or not.

One for Sorrow

Everybody was gazing around confusedly, but I was the only one who really realized there was a presence with us, except maybe for Alexa and Bridget. Bridget shot me a look of worry but I just shook my head, I was sure that there was nothing to worry about. Alexa's eyes darted between us as if she was watching a game of tennis but words failed to leave her scarlet lips.
"Miss Harrington is quite right. However, your main subject of focus is the statue," Mr Geoffries agreed, "Much of our town history is represented by this statue."

      Alexa looked up from where she rested and we all turned to the ancient stone. It had been carved into the simple shape of a cross, for the innocent deaths during the witch trials. On the left side, a magpie was settled, its jaw opened wide as it cawed a remembrance. It was easy to notice that his eyes glowed a deep burgundy colour, something that only just occurred to me, staring into the eyes of the magpie was almost like staring into the soul of the town. Hairs rose upon my arms as a shiver passed down my spine, making my usual solid form shudder.
"What is that carved into the bottom?" Damon enquired, showing his newcomer status to Eastmere.
"That's quite an interesting story. It wasn't originally carved into the statue. Neither was the magpie. The cross was for those lost in the war between the American natives and the Pilgrim Fathers from the United Kingdom. Many think it was for the witch trials but evidence shows it was there long before that. The magpie was added in 1743 after the town was declared

the 'Magpie', after a huge silver yield was found in the cliff. That's why all those caves are there. The town was named that due to having the largest flock of Magpies in America as part of our residence. The engraving, well, no-one's sure about that, but some say," Mr Geoffries paused, lowering his voice, "That a witch made the engraving as a curse upon the town."

    I looked away, feeling a shudder pass through my spine again.

    I wish it was just a myth.

"Adrian?" Bridget questioned as she noticed the look of dread that was written on my face.

***

"Hey, where are you going?" Bridget asked as she caught up to me effortlessly.

    It would have been impressive if she was not what she was. Although, she was not as fast as me, she usually could keep up with me without a problem. Her hair remained motionless against her back as she moved to stand beside me.

"I want to walk away, by myself," I explained.

    I had been away from Eastmere for a long time; I had my reasons but I still had not found what I was searching for, and I could not until the tide went out. It was useless searching during high tide and I had something else I needed to attend to. Bridget seemed to understand my rather uncomfortable state and nodded, already brewing an excuse behind those intoxicating violet eyes for my rather abrupt disappearance. Bridget

One for Sorrow

understood me, I found that the rest of the group did not.
"Right, see you tomorrow?" she asked.
"Of course," I replied with the slight bow of my head.

Bridget smiled before seemingly gliding back to the group. I forgot the conversation I just participated in and cast my attention to the matter in hand. I have accepted my diploma countless times, it was becoming tedious now. As I walked away from the group, I could feel Alexa's piercing eyes in the back of my head. I knew that she wanted me for something but I was not interested in fraternising with women like her, well her type to be specific. I managed to put Alexa to the back of my mind before turning the corner, out of her sight and away from the eyes of my classmates.

Eastmere was not exactly large and as it was surrounded by dense forest, I was standing beside the forest in minutes. My nose signposted the direction, the scent of salt filling my nose as my legs took me closer to the cliff edge. But before I could reach the cliffs, the path for my destination became obviously clear. Never had I seen a clump of trees grown so closely together. Curiosity sparked in my mind and I knew I had to investigate further.

Anna was not the smartest witch out there, then again, the town's people were not the smartest either. I moved the thicket out of my way before sliding through the narrow gap guarded by the cave formation. An eerie feeling washed over my body, it was clear that I was in the correct place. Stalagmites and stalactites were either hanging from the ceiling or growing from the cold hard ground like jagged teeth. An awful musky scent emerged from the depths of the cave like a bad breath, as if the cave were a living being. I had just casually strolled into the beast's mouth, unwittingly making my way down it's throat and into its stomach.

     A wave of air pulsed from the belly of the beast as I moved further. The cave tickled me like a caress, as if Anna's soul was still in the cave and inviting me in. I think a part of her still existed in the caves, lingering because of her anger at the prejudice of the witch hunt and the brutality of the situation we had been placed in. I was sorrowful about that night, it should not have ended that way.

     My legs were more willing than my head as I moved deeper into the beast. The slight breeze intensified and I knew that it was Anna. No normal wind felt like that. Lost words echoed from the walls, the night of her death replaying, voices shouting, screaming and the curse being cast.

     If only it was a myth, but no curse has ever been more real. No curse I had experienced had ever been so powerful. The curse was the only explanation I could give for the strange events that occurred in Eastmere. A magpie crowed, intensifying my awareness and for the first time in a long time I was cautious. I knew what I was trying to find was bigger than me yet I could not walk away. My feet became damp from the sea water which filled part of the cave during high tide. I knew Anna's cave came from the cliff but I did not think the main entrance she used was in the forest. It suddenly became apparent however, especially after all she told me about being one with nature. I struggled to remember the events of that night, and how I ended up in Anna's cave alongside her. I turned my head to the right as I analysed the cave and its contents.

And then I saw them, names carved into the stone of the wall roughly. Seven names all engraved into the beast, one of them being my own. The instinct to fly was taken over by curiosity. I could not understand why it was my name.

My eyes followed the names further until a small gathering of items was visible. It was Anna's cave, her cave, and the book of shadows on the centre of the desk, weathered with age. Everything I needed was right in front of me. Images of the night where everything fell to pieces flashed into my mind and I paused for a minute. I was a different person all of them years ago.

An inhuman roar was released and I whipped around only to be knocked down by a strong figure I knew was not human. As my eyes adjusted, it approached further and a gasp left my lips as I was pushed against the cold stone. A throbbing pain appeared at the back of my head before I was knocked out. My head lolled to one side as I lost sight of surroundings and pain clouded my every thought. The last part of reality faded from my mind but I hung onto the words I read; One for sorrow. Adrian for sorrow.

Chapter Four- Alina

"Do you want to come together for next week's game?" Fizzy asked, pulling her long hair into a high pony tail that sat proudly on top of her head, "Do a huge group dance to get the school riled up?"
"Yeah, might be a good idea," I replied before applying a coat of red lipstick, "I'm sure the seniors will be up for it too."

Fizzy took the tube from me and applied her own coat, puckering her lips shortly after as she admired her appearance in the mirror. I straightened out my own uniform as I glanced down at the black and red colours, with a white logo printed brightly on the front. We had to ask for the red to be placed on; black or white lipstick was not the look the captains wanted for the Eastmere magpies. Both Fizzy and I walked in front of the girls, checking everything was intact. The captain of the junior team, Merissa, was away at a college visit so she had left me in charge of the Junior and senior team. Honestly, I was buzzing, it was a good way for me to show my potential for when they elected next year's captain. It was something I really wanted to add to my application for college later on, I hoped it would help me to stand out.

One for Sorrow

"Lacey, do up your shoes for once please," Fizzy groaned as I came to stand in front of Alexa, finding my arms folding themselves over my chest in disgust. "Pull it down; we're professional, not tacky," I ordered, narrowing my eyes. With Alexa it was imperative to talk to her in a way she seemed to understand, there was no sugar coating anything with her. You had to speak the complete truth or she wouldn't acknowledge your requests.

She rolled her eyes at me before moving her skirt around two inches below her leotard; I guess it was a bit better. Fizzy came up beside me; a smirk playing on her lips as thrill filled her features. "Look who's come to watch," she said in a sing-song voice.

The grin on her face grew wider as I cast a glance to the direction she was beaming at. At the entrance where the cheerleaders would come out from, sat on the benches with Mack a boy from our year was Damon, talking to him half-heartedly as his eyes rested on me.

"From last week of last year girls, start from the beginning!" I instructed and my team all formed a V-shape, me at the top of the point. My girls ran behind me as we entered onto the field, going through our morning practise before school began. The early mornings were always a struggle but I always felt set up for the day after cheer practise. My eyes met Damon's from across the field and his eyes were alight with amusement.

This was going to be a long training session, especially with Damon watching.

One for Sorrow

***

"Girls go clear up!" I ordered and they wandered off, gossiping about the latest news of the school.
"Good session," Fizzy grinned as she grabbed her towel and slung it over her shoulder.
"I know, can't wait to see the homecoming game, you practised enough?" I questioned.
"Feels like it's all I've been doing," Fizzy rolled her eyes, "Ready to see how the electronic violin fits in though."

A magpie cawed, causing for me to jump slightly. I quickly slowed my breathing as I realised it was Eastmere being Eastmere, feeling my frantic heart fade back to its normal speed. The fog that suffocated the forest seemed to lift suddenly as the last dregs of night were invaded by the light of the morning sun. Tipping my pink bottle back, I gulped back half of the bottle of water. A frown pulled at the corner of Bridget's lips as she locked her phone and chucked it onto her gym bag.
"What's wrong?" I questioned.
"No news," Bridget muttered, "I think I'm going to skip next period and go see if he's okay."
"I'm sure he is," I reassured.
"Adrian doesn't have parents, he lives alone, I just want to make sure," I could see the concern laced in her expression and knew there was no chance of dissuading her, "It's just there's no-one at home with him so if something happened there would be no-one there for him. I just need to know he's okay."

"He'll be fine Bridget," Alexa shook her head at Bridget's concern, her pony tail swinging behind her head.

"You don't get it do you," Bridget was starting to get angry, "He has insomnia, he doesn't sleep at night and quite often we end up talking in the night. Me not hearing from him means there's something definitely wrong."

There was something behind Bridget's concern that was evident. It wasn't just worry for a friend; her level of fear was for something much more but I couldn't quite put my finger on it.

"I'm going either way guys, I don't really care about maths anyway," Bridget rolled her eyes dramatically, something she refrained from doing usually.

"I don't think you need to," Alexa shook Bridget's shoulder roughly, causing her to scowl.

But her scowl quickly changed as our eyes landed on Adrian. He staggered onto the field, both Bridget and I broke into a sprint, rushing forward, and rested him up on us. I felt my body drop as he leant all his weight on the both of us and I strained to move him towards the benches. His breathing was staggered and I noticed the pallor in his skin was much deeper than usual, almost as if the life was being drained from him.

"What happened?" I asked, setting him down on one of the benches painfully.

"I'm not sure, my head hurts, I was-"

"Did someone hit you over the head?" I questioned.

"I-"

He frowned in confusion and the expression on his face caused me to worry. There was something not right about Adrian, I had never seen him like that. His eyes were wide as he stared around at the environment he was in and the people he was with with a look of vulnerability to them, almost like a doe caught in the headlights. Vulnerable was never a word I had associated with Adrian until today. I looked to Bridget who seemed to be holding her breath as she looked to our friend with worry.

"I think you need to go to get checked over," I suggested.

Damon nodded in agreement with me and heaved him up.

"Hey Mack! Help us out, would you?" I called waving the guy over, "Take him to medical please."

Mack nodded, pulling Adrian's arm over his shoulder to help Damon in taking him to medical. Bridget gave me a worried glance before hauling her gym bag onto her shoulder and following the boys. They began walking towards the school with Damon and Mack supporting a staggering Adrian.

"What happened?" Fizzy asked, jogging over.

"I'm not sure. Adrian just appeared from nowhere with something that seemed like concussion," I explained, turning to get my bag.

I noticed that Alexa had walked away, her ponytail swaying in time with her steps as she almost marched towards the other end of the field and towards the forest. A frown filled my lips but I shrugged it off, Alexa was no concern of mine.

"Is he going to be okay?" Fizzy questioned, my attention averting back towards her.

Shrugging, I replied, "I'm not sure to be honest, we best check on him in medical."

Both of us trudged across the field and up the stairs onto the next floor, walking down the corridor as the sun beamed through the windows onto us. Fizzy's hair was molten in the sunlight and her crystal blue eyes twinkled gorgeously. The corridors were silent as everyone had made their way to next lesson already. It was eerie to see the school like it currently was, it was almost as if everything was gone and Fizzy and I were the only two left on the planet. We wondered down the corridor, no words were passed between us. When we arrived, Adrian was staring at a cup of water in what appeared to be despair. He seemed confused as if he was a lost puppy in the darkest of storms. His expression was bewildered and he appeared so vulnerable. A shudder passed down my spine, I didn't like to see my friend like this.

"Adrian, are you okay?" I bent down to his level as the nurse stepped in.

He looked pale, paler than usual and he was breathing heavily through his mouth as if he was in great pain. His eyes looked dark and feral, but with an inner struggle. I felt like I needed to wrap him in my embrace and just tell him that everything was going to be okay but that didn't feel like it was going to be enough. Adrian was lost somewhere deep in his mind and he had no way of escaping the prison he had built himself.

"I-" he took a deep shuddering breath, causing his body to tremble, "I haven't eaten today."

One for Sorrow

A grim smile cracked his lips and a steely determination took over him.
"Do you want me to get you something from the canteen?" Bridget suggested as she took his hand.
Something flashed between them, a knowing look passing through both their eyes. I failed to say anything and just watched as they continue to converse through a silent conversation.
"No, I need a drink," he whispered with a strained voice.
I looked down to the cup of water in confusion as he passed it to Bridget who left it abandoned on the side, untouched.
"Can you walk?" Bridget asked.
"Yeah," he coughed, struggling to his feet.
Bridget pulled him up and they left together. Fizzy and I headed to our next class, separating as she moved to join her own class. I fumbled over an apology to the teacher but he just brushed it off, my reputation doing wonders for my tardiness. A few minutes later, Alexa sauntered into the class, without an apology and sank down slowly into the seat next to me. Teacher just gave her a sideways glance and just returned his attention back to his whiteboard. In front of us, Harry turned around and passed Alexa a note. She took it, read it, and scribbled one word before handing it back. I watched as Harry's glimmer of hope sank back into the earth's core and burned to ash.
"I heard about Adrian," she whispered, "What did he say to the nurse?"
The teacher glanced our way but didn't say anything. Alexa flashed him a sultry smile and he

turned his back away from the class again to continue teaching algorithms.
She continued, "Is he going to be okay?"

My eyes glanced towards the teacher, ensuring it was safe before turning back to Alexa.
"I'm not sure, Bridget took him to get a drink," I replied and her eyes hardened.
"What kind of drink?" she questioned.
"I don't know, juice or something," I shot back.
"Girls!" the teacher lectured with his voice and I gave him an apologetic smile.

Alexa gave her own smile before turning back to the front, an expression of thinking on her face.
"What's going on? Why did she want to know what kind of drink she was getting him?" Damon asked, "Surely it doesn't matter, it's just a drink."
"I don't know," I expressed honestly with a slight shrug to my shoulders.

***

(Adrian)

"Are you okay now?" Bridget asked me, her eyes filled with worry.

I did not answer for a couple of seconds as I stared into her faerie eyes. They glazed over in worry when I did not give her a reply. My head was still a little fuzzy and I struggled to formulate words with my mouth.
"I should be okay," I answered, speaking slowly as my eyes glanced to the empty flask that sat in between us, "You will have to thank your father for me."

"Of course," she nodded her head.

Bridget wore her expression on her face as curiosity filled her features. I knew what she was going to ask but I did not know what kind of answer I would give her.

"Adrian, what were you doing?" she asked, "You were so weak, you are so weak, that shouldn't have happened."

I looked down at my hands as thoughts clouded my mind, but not the right ones. As hard as I tried to remember, I just could not and a frown spread across my face. Bridget shuffled so she was facing me and took my hand in hers. She sat with her legs folded beneath her, her knees brushing against mine. I could feel the heat from her body radiate onto mine, the heat from her living body. If I could feel anything I knew electric shocks would radiate from her hands onto mine but I could not. For now, I would have to relish in the comfort of her warmth.

"What do you remember last?" she enquired and I opened my mouth to speak but closed it immediately, the thought had left me.

"I-"

"Adrian, something's very wrong here," she began, "Have you met someone or something?"

"Something happened," I muttered, rubbing my head as if I had banged it.

"We last saw you at the group history project, and you told me you had to do something, that was yesterday," I stretched out slightly as she spoke and she suddenly shot backwards, "Urgh!"

One for Sorrow

Bridget grimaced and began to frantically fan her nose. My lips frowned in confusion and she held her nose as she looked at me funnily.

"What?" I asked, a curious laugh bubbling in my throat at her overreaction to nothing.

"You reek of manticore," she raised an eyebrow, "I thought I smelt it on the field but I thought I must have imagined it."

"A manticore…" I echoed, trying to recall ever meeting one of those but then it hit me, "I found Anna's cave."

"You what?!" Bridget gave me an incredulous look, her purple eyes wide and searching.

"It isn't in the cliffs. I have been searching for decades, but there's nothing there, so I began searching the woods on the edge, and I found it."

"Where abouts?"

"Sorry?" modern language confused me.

"Where is it located?" Bridget rolled her eyes.

"I-"I shut my mouth again suddenly, I didn't know where it was, I had forgotten.

I deserved to be hung, drawn, and quartered at that moment. It was almost as unbelievable as the revelation of the supernatural world! How had I forgotten where her cave was? Bridget's eyes were still searching me, bright and wide, showing her every innocence and curiosity.

"It was in a dense area, really overgrown. The forest somewhere," I tried to form some clarity in my head. "We need to go, at the end of the week-"

"Shouldn't you two be in class?" A teacher walked up to us, amusement causing his lips to curl upwards.

"I am sorry sir, I was just collecting some work from my locker with Bridget," I explained giving him an apologetic smile.
"I shall escort you two back to class," the teacher announced, "Are you in the same class?"
"Yes," I replied.
"Let's go children!"

I had to supress the laugh that had formed in my throat, I was much older than him. Both of us followed the teacher who was wider than he was tall. The door swung open with a creak and Bridget and I found our seats without looking at the class. Alexa shot me a look with her eyes and I nodded as a confirmation that it was what she was thinking. Alexa and I did not like what the other was much but we still had enough respect to look out for each other. Bridget's elegant fingers tickled my hand under the table as she tried to stay in contact with me. She knew I was in a vulnerable place currently and I was thankful for her staying with me. Without thinking, I licked my fangs, making sure they were clean. Alina was giving me a strange look as if she was trying to connect two and two together. Things in Eastmere were changing, especially with the revelation of Anna's cave.

Chapter Five- Alina

"What's up sis?" I questioned as we settled on a bench next to each other, I could tell from the look of dismay on her face that something was wrong.
"Not a lot, just struggling with this physics homework," she sighed.
"You'll get there, I know you will," I gave her a sideways hug and she just smiled brightly.
"I know, just a bit bummed I had to cancel on Reece and Chad tonight, they invited me to their rehearsals, I just know that I won't get the work done if I went over," she frowned.
"It'll be worth it in the end," I told her and she nodded.
"I love having you as a sister sometimes," Fizzy grinned up at me and I smiled.
"Me too," I spoke and then I retested my words, "I mean, love having you as a sister. Wow that sounded weird."

Fizzy just giggled joyously at me, any worries about her physics homework suddenly disappeared. She spotted Chad and Reece in the distance and waved to them. Both of their faces lit up at the sight of her and she gave me a quick squeeze before bounding away. I rose from my position on the bench carefully, ensuring my backpack didn't topple me over. My legs began to walk towards the exit of the school through the high black gates that towered above me. A long sigh left my lips at the weight of the bag on my shoulder and knew the long walk that was ahead of me. "Hey Alina, wait up!" My body turned around to see Damon running towards me.

I stopped, shrugging my backpack into a more comfortable position as it was beginning to become more painful. My chest expanded as I took in a deep breath in attempt to calm myself down before he reached me. I almost hated the way he made me feel, it was unfamiliar territory for me and I felt like I was walking into the unknown. One wrong step and it was all over and anything I currently felt for Damon could be forgotten almost instantly as if it had never happened. I mentally shook my head at myself, I couldn't believe how dramatic I was being.
"Here, let me carry that," Damon held out his arm demandingly for my backpack.

Cautiously I handed him my backpack, waiting for him to run off laughing and pour the contents of my bag onto the ground like half the junior class would. Instead, he shouldered my bag and smiled widely as he walked beside me. We took slow strides out of school as students rushed past us, excited to get home after the stress of the school day.

The sky was a clear, crystal blue which was unusual for Eastmere. A gentle breeze caused the trees to make a monotone rustling like thousands of birds taking off at the same time. A bird cawed and threw itself into the air, gliding into the depths of the clouds until it had left my sight. It was almost as if the

weather in Eastmere was playing to my mood and was urging for good fortune to occur with Damon.
"Have you had a good week?" I questioned.
"Yeah, I feel like I'm sort of starting to get used to the school a bit, everyone's been really friendly. Feel like I got lucky being paired with you because you know so many people," Damon laughed.
I just shrugged my shoulders, "I know a lot of people but I keep my inner circle small but close."
"Anyway, where are you heading?" he questioned, smiling down at me.

    I couldn't help but notice the way his shirt hugged his body, suggesting at the muscles that rippled underneath. There was something about Damon that made me question everything I had come to understand about boys. I was thankful to be questioned, it showed there was something new around, something that was worth changing my opinion for.
"I was heading to Mag's pie place to hang out with some people from school before the game tonight," my arms felt awkward hanging by my side with nothing to carry as I spoke to him, "It's usually where the cheerleaders and the football players go before the game. You know? Gets us riled up for a fight. I'm not sure if I'm going tonight though, seniors are cheering and I have a lot of chemistry work to prep for."
"Where's that?"
"It's a diner on Second Street, not far," I added, "They do the best strawberry milkshakes ever. I bet you've never tasted anything like it."
"I'll have to try one," I smiled up at him and he grinned, revealing prefect white teeth like shiny pearls

lined up in a row, it was almost as if there was nothing I could fault with him.

"It was a little weird with Adrian today," he began and I nodded my head in agreement.

He was right, it was a bit strange but he didn't understand that things like that happened all the time in this town. Even I had to admit that Adrian's case today was a bit of an anomaly for Eastmere, especially as it was daylight. As weird as it was I had never considered it dangerous, but with the state Adrian was in, I was beginning to consider it. I made a mental to note to make sure I checked with Adrian that he was doing okay when I next saw him; and Bridget for that matter, she was really worried.

"Yeah, I guess so," I admitted.

"You say that this town isn't what it seems," he started, "What do you mean by that?"

Just as he spoke those words we rounded the corner onto the street. I left his answer hanging for a few moments as we approach the brightly lit diner, the white paint stark as it gleamed in the sunlight. Damon opened the glass door for me which I smiled at brightly, ready to answer his question now we were inside.

"I-" I closed my mouth as I approached the counter and ordered two milkshakes, Damon passing over a note before I could find my purse, "You didn't have to do that?"

"Well, I wanted to," he smiled at me again and I couldn't help but smile back at him.

He just had one of those smiles that could put my own onto my face on the darkest of days. Damon grabbed the tray and I lead him towards the black booths in the corner, away from prying eyes from school. I knew the rumours that would fly around and I didn't want to encourage them, people were always quick to assume. My eyes glanced out of the window and into the depths of the forest, a shiver passing down my spine. I took my cool glass of pink and took a sip; Damon followed and let out a groan of pleasure at the taste.

"So good," he mumbled before sipping another mouthful.

"I told you they were the best," I laughed, a teasing tone to my voice.

A small giggle left my lips and a short blonde waitress approached us. I smiled to welcome her as she stood before us, a portion of fries resting on the ruby red tray.

"From the young lady at the bar," she placed a portion of fries in between us.

My head turned to see Fizzy winking at me suggestively. Damon laughed and I shifted my attention back to him.

"Dunking fries in milkshake is kind of my thing," I blushed, "Fizzy clearly just wants to embarrass me."

"I do it too, and ice cream," Damon shrugged, demonstrating as he took one of the longer fries and dunked it into the pink froth.

I supressed a giggle as I shook my head, following his lead as we tucked into the fries. There was something about the contrast of the salt of the fries and the sweet of the milkshake that was heaven to me. It had the best of both worlds. I glanced at Damon quickly through my eyelashes, watching the absent-minded smile that filled his features. He looked happy but I had no way to gauge if he was feeling the same way that I was.

"You were talking about the town," he offered as a reminder and I nodded, thankful for the topic of conversation.

"Erm, I've been here my whole life and strange things always happen," I explained, "Especially at night. I'm not superstitious or anything like that but just don't go out at night by yourself or at least stick to the roads that have street lamps on them. It's almost as if it's when the bad stuff comes out to play."

"Really?" he drawled and my eyes found a magpie looking directly at us, "Like what?"

The magpie stared at me hungrily with its red eyes and I was quickly becoming creeped out by it. I placed the crazy straw between my dry lips and took a sip of fruity goodness to try and distract myself from its stare, reminding myself of how good it was.

"Did you know that Eastmere is known for its population of Magpies?" I offered and his eyes found the bird almost immediately.

Both of us watched as the magpie spread its wings as it took off to the sky. I diverted my attention back to Damon and tried to shake off any thoughts of the magpie that I had.

"I don't really know what I'm talking about," I forced a laugh, "I've been here all my life, it's probably quite normal."

"Well the gym teacher seemed a little strange," he frowned as if trying to remember something.

"Did you get stuck with Mr Jones?" I smirked, a laugh bubbling inside me.

"Yeah…"

I burst out laughing, unable to contain it anymore.

"What?" he was so cute when he was confused.

I pushed him playfully with him still frowning.

"So, what were you saying about the magpies?" he asked, slipping his hand into mine and curling his fingers around my own.

A flutter passed through my chest, making me shiver.

"Are you cold?" he asked, wrapping an arm around my shoulders and pulling me closer.

Being so close made me shiver more, but not from the cold. A guy has never managed to make me feel this way before and I was in an entirely new territory. I had to pause and think about what I was saying for a moment, I had known him mere hours in the grand scheme of life, it had been six days since I met him. It was like an enchantment. Knowing Eastmere, it felt like anything was possible.

"Just a chill," I lied, using it as an excuse to lean into his invitingly warm chest.

A sigh escaped my lips as a sense of pulsing warmth spread through my body; it was pleasant and completing.

"Hey, are you…" Damon trailed off in a dreamy tone.

"What?" my eyebrows furrowed in confusion.

"Nothing, it's just…" slowly he leant in, the smell of his strawberry breath hitting my nose.

One for Sorrow

Naturally, I held my breath as he held his face inches away from my own. Just as I was about to seal the deal, Fizzy jumped next to me.
"Come on guys, you just met!" she giggled and she leapt away when I moved to hit her, "Reece is playing! I need five bucks."

Fizzy smiled expectantly as she held her hand out. I sighed, pulling out a ten-dollar bill and placing it in her hand. She gleamed and did a mocking curtsy. I grinned as she skipped back towards the bar to get Reece his usual before a show. I knew she had a crush on Reece, so being the good sister that I was; I let her go watch him play every time, and get his food, that way she had a reason to talk to him.
"She seems...nice," Damon grinned at me.
"You don't have to live with her. She's more hyperactive then a dog in heat on caffeine."

Damon laughed, chuckling low in his throat. "Come on, I'll show you the den," I offered, standing up and giving him my hand to lead him away from the booth and our empty glasses.
"I love how she bought us fries and then asked for some dollars," Damon laughed.
"That's Fizzy for you," I shook my head.

The den was basically the largest red booth in Mag's pie place. It was round the back of the restaurant where all the teenagers went after school. Mrs Maguire, the owner set it up to keep the rowdy bunch away from her other customers, that way it kept everyone happy. It's supposed to sit around twelve people, but there was usually at least fifteen of us. Fizzy had saved us a space near Bridget who was sat

One for Sorrow

very closely to Adrian. Alexa was shooting Bridget glares from across the table from her perch on a new victim's lap. His name tag read Lance and he reminded me of a young Thor with long shaggy blonde hair and a well-muscled body. He was hot; the kind of guy Alexa would go for, probably a football player. He wore a 'Denvington Devils' school shirt, which meant he would be playing in the first game for the state cup later. The rest of his team was sat around two booths on the other side of the diner, laughing, shouting and getting wired up for the game.

Music was coursing through the air, a dull thudding that tickled my feet. The Eastmere Magpies banner had been hung above the main bar. Mrs Maguire was stood pouring two sodas for a couple of sophomore girls. She usually stayed amongst the teenagers at this time, she said it was because it made her feel young again to see us all.

"Hello there, Alina! Who's this?" Mrs Maguire smirked knowingly at Damon, whose attention had been drawn to the Denvington Devils.

I nudged his arm, bringing him back into the room.

"Er, I'm Damon," he smiled charmingly.

"You can call me Sharon," Mrs Maguire replied as she passed us two large strawberry milkshakes, "Reece is playing later, you stayin'?"

Reece was Sharon's nephew but was more like her son. She always seemed to glow when she spoke of him.

"Of course," I smiled, taking a milkshake.

"In which case, you're going to have to pay for those, I don't want them youngens finding out I've been giving away freebies," Sharon raised an eyebrow.

Damon gave me a look as if asking whether she was serious and I nodded. He wearily handed over a note. Mrs Maguire took the note with a smirk and waved us over towards our group.

"And tell that sister of yours Reece is playin' somethin' special," she said with a wink before turning to her next customer, "Can I help you, hun?"

"She didn't give me any change," Damon frowned as he stuffed his wallet back into his pocket.

"You didn't ask for it," I grinned, taking a sip of strawberry milky goodness.

He chuckled and shook his head at me before taking a sip of his own drink. This was our second in mere hours but I had no complaints, I could drink these all day.

"Are you going to the game?" he questioned and I looked over to my sister.

Reece had his arm wrapped protectively around her shoulder as she mumbled something into his chest which he laughed at.

"No, she stole the rest of my money and the seniors are cheering tonight so I'm not needed," I laughed and he shook his head.

"I don't really want to go anyway, it seems as if half of the town would be there," he stated

"More like the whole town," I laughed and he nodded.

I noticed Bridget and Adrian slip away from the group, walking close together but not close enough for someone to notice. A frown spread across my lips,

pulling my features downwards. It was unusual for Bridget to leave without saying goodbye to me.
"Do you fancy going for a walk with me?" he asked and I smiled, two dimples forming on my cheeks.
"Yeah, I'd love that," I agreed and he wrapped his arm around my shoulder like Reece had Fizzy.

    Damon gave me a sense of completion, something I appreciated. Eastmere was changing for me, and for once, I welcomed a change.

Chapter Six- Adrian

"Adrian, are you sure you want to go back in?" Bridget turned, her concerned eyes found my own as she did.

A shaky sigh left my lips but I nodded my head almost confidently. Anna's cave might be the key to everything, we had to go back, especially since I had located the book of shadows. I knew where Anna had taken the curse from and that book had the key to figuring out the towns fate.

"Let's go," I urged and she nodded.

Carefully Bridget stepped around the growing stalagmites and stalactites and I followed a bit more swiftly. She paused at the entrance, allowing her eyes to adjust to the shift in lighting. I could see her nose wrinkle as she sensed the air as if she was searching for something, or someone.

"What is it?" I whispered in her ear.

She shivered at the sound of my voice before turning to face me.

"I'm not sure, I can't smell the manticore but I don't know where it would be, shall we move out or-"

"Come on, we need the book of shadows," I pushed her on further and she gave me a reluctant nod.

For a faerie and with the power she had, I thought she would be a bit more confident. I grabbed her hand and she shot me a grateful smile. My body

guided her deeper into the cave before her features screwed up in disgust. She pinched her nose again as she released my hand from our lock and fanned her nose dramatically again. I did not have to ask her what she had smelt, I knew what it was almost immediately.
"That is manticore," the sound of her voice changed due to the blockage of her nasal passage, causing me to chuckle lightly.
"He's probably resting, it was not long ago he fought with me," I explained and she nodded.
"We need to be quick," she pressed and I agreed with a swift nod.

She cautiously ventured further into the darkness but my feet were sure against the hard floor. As we moved deeper, the aura began to change and I became more cautious. I was sure this was where we needed to be, the ghost of Anna seemingly filled me. She was still present in these caves. I could smell the manticore's fowl fur from here, but could tell it was much deeper in the cave depths. I had a feeling we would not be able to avoid a second meeting with the beast.
"Do you think you could use your magic?" I asked, helping Bridget over a boulder.

I knew she did not need my help, faeries were one of the most agile beings however I just wanted a reason to hold her hand.
"I don't know, I don't like it here. There's too much bad magic down here. It doesn't feel good," Bridget murmured, ducking under a stalagmite.

I did not understand what she was saying. Anna was adamant when she was convincing me of her healing powers that she meant no harm. I could not understand why Bridget would sense bad magic if all Anna did was heal things.

"The curse," a whisper of realisation left my lips.

"What?" Bridget's brow furrowed in confusion.

"The curse, that's the bad magic," I stated.

"I don't want to admit it but I believe so," she gave a sorry look before walking ahead of me.

"We need to find a way to stop the curse," I stressed.

"How can we stop something we do not understand, that is an impossible task at the moment," Bridget shook her head.

"The book of shadows will tell us more if that's where the curse originated from," I confirmed.

    A breeze blew through the cave, but it came from inside the cave, like a warning. Bridget shivered, but being what I was, I was unmoved. Bridget glanced at me, I knew she had seen the expression on my face and it was predictable what she was about to say next.

"What you are is a gift," she smiled towards me, taking my hand.

"A gift can be taken back," I whispered, moving past her.

"You're not cursed Adrian," Bridget insisted.

    Her purple eyes pleaded with my own, catching the light from a crack in the roof of the cave. I leaned down to brush my lips against hers. She responded and slipped her hand into mine.

"Then what am I?" I whispered into her ear as I pulled away from her soft lips, "I am a monster of the night, sucking the life force from breathing, living creatures to remain undead. I shalt not preserve this existence if it were not for you bringing the light back into my soul."

"Adrian," Bridget shushed me with another brush of our lips, "You're slipping into old English again."

She smiled, drawing me behind her and I sighed.

"What am I supposed to do? I am not right for this world anymore," I bent down to slip through a particularly narrow gap.

"You are, Adrian. If you were not supposed to be here, you would already be dead," Bridget stopped still in her tracks, "Why won't you talk about the past?"

"What do you mean? With Anna?" I frowned.

"No, like what did you do for three hundred years, did you ever fall in love again, friends? You must have done something? What made you come back?"

"Well, I did a lot, I travelled most of the time, kept moving from one place to the other constantly. I did not want to stay in one place for long, I did not want to get attached," I explained.

"That must have been lonely," Bridget gave me a sympathetic look as we ventured onwards.

"I guess, I only came back because I saw a picture of Felicity in the newspaper when I was one town over, thought it was Anna, scared me to begin with so I came to investigate," I explained and Bridget nodded her head in understanding.

"The beast is close," the air around us grew cold and Bridget shivered, her whole body shaking from the bitter temperature.

"I'm going to cast a veil around us, hopefully, the manticore has not yet sensed us," she placed a hand on my shoulder tenderly.

"And I am the one slips into ye ol'english?"

Bridget smirked as she began murmuring under her in the old language of the Fey. A light breeze picked up around us, tugging at our clothes and hair as if it intended on making us bare. The breeze became wind to a gale, almost knocking me into a stalagmite that touched the ground. I hissed, feeling my fangs slip down from my gums. I hated my fangs; I bit my lips and tasted my own blood. It was sour and dead, making me feel ill and my stomach turned at it like a pit of snakes. I spat it out before my demon had chance to rise like a snake slithering up my throat.

A low rumble of sound echoed from the cave depths. The manticore had sensed something was there that shouldn't be.

"Bridget-"I warned.

"The veil should protect us. I have sent a shade to lure the beast away," she explained, "This way."

I followed her down a dark passage. The cave was not what I expected or what I remembered. It scared me how little I remembered from the night before. A strange sense filled me as we took careful steps deeper into the depths of the beast. I knew I was already deeper than I was yesterday evening; I must have wounded the manticore badly.

Apart from the fungal scent of the beast, the cave smelled fresh, not the usual dark, mouldy smell associated with caves. There was an undertone of dried herbs too. Everything my senses picked up told me that

this was Anna's cave, as well as the heavy feeling in my stomach that seemingly weighed me down.
"We must be close now," I decided ducking under a wooden beam.
"Don't be fooled. I wouldn't put it past Anna to leave a few false trails."
"No look," I pointed to a symbol of a magpie with its wings spread, "that is her sign."
"Well, let's not wait around then," she said but her voice was tinged with nervousness.
"We go in, grab the book and leave."
"Sounds good to me," Bridget rolled her shoulders.
"Do you want me to go first?" I suggested.
"I thought you were a gentleman," she smiled but stood to the side and let me pass.

The smell of herbs was stronger now, but it was washed out by a sulphurous scent and dried roses. Something was telling me to run and never look back but the book was in there. It was something that I had to do, it was calling to me. Carefully, I inched forward into the darkness and I heard Bridget release a huff of breath.
"Hurry up, we can't be long," Bridget shouted in a whisper and I shook my head.

My head darted around in search of the book but the place was littered with spell books. I could not remember where it was from the night before, the area of the cave was untouched but yet it didn't seem stagnant, as if someone had been here recently, since the night everything changed. I knew Anna would not leave something so precious lying around, she was smarter than that. She was educated, well read and very protective over what mattered to her most. That was why the cave was well concealed because no ordinary person would look at the growth pattern of trees. Thankfully, I was not ordinary.

"Got it!" Bridget exclaimed, a smile filling her lips. She stood over an oak table, removing a veil that surrounded the book to pick it up, "Anna shrouded it away."

"That is why I could sense it but not find it," I muttered in realisation but yet for some reason, it felt like I had seen it last night. It was almost as if Anna was still here and cast the spell just yesterday after I was gone.

"Bridget, I think Anna's spirit is still with us, I can sense her," I whispered.

"Well let's not stick around then, do not be fooled into thinking she would be happy to see either of us, including you," Bridget shot back.

I turned around to exit, it was making me want to shiver with the atmosphere in this cave, something glistening caught my eye. I moved towards it, almost in a daze. It was hypnotic, mesmerising.

"Adrian, we have to go! What are you… oh, that's lovely," she whispered, standing next to me so that our shoulders touched.

The medallion glittered gold in the dim lighting. Bridget reached out to touch it, picked it up with the carefulness of a mother lifting her new born child, then pulled her arm back abruptly.

"Ouch!" she screamed, dropping the medallion, and cursing in the language of the Fey.

"That things gold," she muttered, coming out of her daze.

Thankfully, her scream had brought me back to the present.

"Let me," I said, picking up the medallion into my hand and then into my coat pocket, "You have the book?" Bridget nodded in confirmation, "Then we shall go."

A sudden roar filled the cavern; it was like thunder had barged inside, making the walls shudder from the sheer force of it. Dust fell from the ceiling into Bridget's hair. We both paused for a moment, glancing at each other uneasily as the look in our eyes confirmed what the others was thinking.

"It is this way-"I turned, knowing we had to move but came face to face with the manticore.

The front of the creature was a lion, with thickly muscled shoulders, almost bulging. It had a bushy mane of fur that had been bleached grey with age and lack of natural light. Its tail was lifted into strike position. Venom dripped from its scorpion tail menacingly. The manticore made no sign that he was going to move so silently, both Bridget and I stepped back. She held her breath in her lungs, her eyes glancing at the escape every now and again, debating if we could make it without being harmed. I thought we were going to make it but the beast released another frightening roar.

"Run," she screamed.

I probably would have been able to make it out within seconds but I could not leave Bridget behind, that would be unfair of me. I also needed her, she is the only one who truly understands me.

Memories swarmed dangerously in my head as the last visit to Anna's cave appeared from the corner of my mind. Words, words roughly carved into the hard stone of the wall but my memories were lost of the content. I am unsure of what really happened that night, it was possible that was just a dream and that something in Eastmere wanted me to find the caves again.

"Bridget," I gasped as the smell of manticore filled my senses.

Her eyes found mine in alarm before we took off running again in the other direction. The walls flew past us but my eyes failed to find the words. One glance back found the manticore lunging towards us but quickly I shoved Bridget out of the way, landing with a soft thump.

The sound of rocks falling filled my ears and I shielded Bridget's body with my own. Her body shook under me from the fright and the cold of my own body. Soon enough we came back up to check the change in our surroundings. I looked back to find the manticore trapped on the other side of the fallen rocks. We were safe and we had what we came for.

"Still got the book?" I asked and she nodded.

"Still got the medallion?" she checked and I nodded as I patted my jacket pocket.

"You have dust in your hair," Bridget smirked, kneeling in front of me.

She began brushing my hair, but used it as an excuse to connect our lips. As she did, I released a sigh of anguish. Bridget's heart hammered against my chest. Her breath came in short soft pants.

    My heart was still.
    I wasn't breathing.
    I was a monster.

Chapter Seven- Alina

"So, you and Damon huh?" Bridget smirked from her air bed.

She was dressed up in her leopard print onesie and snuggled under various blankets. Bridget was always one for being a cold, I swear I had never heard her complain she was hot unless it was a heatwave.

"Oh my god, did you see her at Mag's Pie Place? She was all like 'glaaaargh?'" Felicity erupted into giggles.

I blushed bright red and swatted at her whilst Bridget grinned. Felicity yelped and dived off the bed, landing on my fluffy rug with a soft thud. She just looked at me before laughing again.

"Are you together then?" Fizzy enquired, leaning forward to rest her head against the bed.

"No!" We met like-" I glanced at the digital clock on my bedside table, "Six days ago!"

"Come on, Alina. You haven't drooled over a guy like that since One Direction."

"I was twelve," I rolled my eyes.

"So? They are a bunch of pretty hot guys," Fizzy shrugged.

"You sound like Alexa," Bridget laughed, pulling the covers over her head to protect herself from Fizzy's attack.

"Hey! That tickles," Bridget shouted, although she was muffled by the thickness of the blankets.

I couldn't help but release a giggle as I looked at my best friend and sister. Fizzy's blonde curls bounced behind her as she loomed over Bridget who was squirming under her tickling hands with laughter erupting from me. Soon enough, Fizzy ended her attack and retreated, I shook my head at them and Bridget gave me a bright grin.

"He did compliment you on the violin at the beginning of the week though Fiz," Bridget pointed out.

"Oh yeah, he said he heard you playing but couldn't find where it was coming from," I concluded.

"That's sweet, I like him," Fizzy laughed joyously before turning to Bridget, "What about you and Adrian?"

"What about us?" she frowned.

"Aren't you interested in each other? You disappeared together straight after our get together at Mag's pie place, missed the game and turned up here covered in dust, late, where did you go?" Fizzy asked me.

Bridget's eyes found mine and we exchanged a look. I turned to Fizzy and shook my head to say don't bother but Bridget spoke anyway, "No, Adrian and I are just friends. He was here with his family years ago when he was young and he's trying to find a cave he used to walk with his family but some rocks fell and blocked our entrance."

Bridget was still under her duvet, half hiding. Her dark, navy eyes peered at me and I couldn't tell what emotions she was hiding.

One for Sorrow

"He was here when he was younger?" Fizzy frowned, I didn't know that either, I don't remember his name or face from when we were younger.
"Yeah, but when he was like really young which is why he doesn't remember it very well," Bridget concluded before turning to Fizzy with a smile toying on her lips, "Anyway, what about you and Reece?"
"He spoke to me and sat next to me and Mrs Maguire told me he was dedicating a song to someone in the audience," Fizzy grinned shyly.
"Did she say who?"
"She winked at me"
"Ah," I nodded as I watched her features grow into a smile.
"He's good though isn't he?" Fizzy continued, her eyes taking on a dreamy look, "He's such a good performer."
"Yeah, I-"
She cut me off, "He's just so, and he make me feel so, and he looks so-"
"Finished sentences please," I laughed and Fizzy's eyes gleamed in laughter, she was completely love struck.
"Okay, he's indescribable," she concluded "You can't talk, you and Damon are the same."
"Finally, something that makes sense," Bridget cheered and I chucked my pillow at her.

      The channel flashed over and Fizzy squealed in delight. She jumped to her feet and landed with her legs beneath her in front of the TV. Her eyes were wide as she absorbed the contents of the whole screen. Thor flashed on and my eyes immediately glued

themselves onto the screen. It was funny to see Fizzy this way, it was only ever when she spoke about Reece or saw an image of Christ Hemsworth that she seemed to change persona into a typical love-struck teenage girl.
"Chris Hemsworth is just so-"Fizzy drawled.
"You're doing it again," I giggled, "But I do get where you're coming from."
  Bridget nodded in agreement eagerly. Her phone began to ring and she looked at the caller ID with a smile on her lips.
"Yeah," she answered in a casual tone.
  Her navy eyes gleamed as the second person in the conversation answered. Her lips tugged at her features until they turned into a wider smile and I could take an educated guess at who was on the other end.
"Really?" she whispered.
"Okay Bridget?" I asked and she nodded but a frown still invaded the smile that she was wearing.
"Not on your own, just wait," she pleaded but an argument was formed, "Please."
  After some small words, she hung up and turned her attention back to the screen, a puzzled look remained in her eyes. Fizzy and I exchanged a glance before turning our attention back to Chris Hemsworth. I knew not to push it from the confusion she was holding in her expression, I wasn't sure she could give me an answer to the question I wanted to ask.
"He got voted this year's sexiest," Fizzy grinned.
"You've only told me, like-" I began counting on my fingers for emphasis, "Seventeen times!"

One for Sorrow

She gave me a sheepish grin before sinking down into the spot she was sitting in. Bridget and I shook our heads in mock disappointment. The conflict in her eyes was evident despite the joyful glint that invaded her eyes but I didn't want to press her for information. I could see the discomfort when Fizzy asked her about Adrian. Bridget was lying about what was going on between her and Adrian but I wasn't sure she really knew herself. I wondered quickly whether I'd be able to find anything out at the pool party tomorrow.

"Adrian, hey," I smiled as I opened the door wider for him, "Go on through, Bridget's setting up the drinks, I'm sure she wants some help."
"Thanks," he mumbled with a small smile on his face.
He slid past me through the door and I was about to close it when I spotted Damon coming up the pathway with Chad, one of Fizzy's friends.
"Hey," I grinned as I saw him, "Go on through Chad, Fizzy's pumping up the pool floats."
"Cool," he smiled as he moved past me like Adrian had, his afro bouncing as he walked.
"Chad had to bring me in," Damon admitted, "And I still have no idea how we got here, your house is literally in the middle of nowhere."
I released a small laugh at his comment. It was true, my nearest neighbours were Damon and Chad and they still lived about a mile and a half away. We liked being the only people in the area, it gave us a sense of freedom although nights could get particularly

spooky at times. Gently, I closed the door to behind Damon and led him through the house. A mass of golden fur bounded towards us as she launched herself at Damon.
"Sunny," I scolded but Damon just stumbled back before beginning to laugh.

He scratched her behind her ears and her eyes closed in appreciation. A small smile twitched onto my lips as I petted Sunny on her head, shaking my head at how needy she was. She jumped down with a little bark before bouncing off towards the next person, her tail swinging from left to right excitedly.
"She's cute," Damon grinned and I nodded in agreement.
"Follow me," I instructed with a smile before stepping out of the patio doors and into the garden.

The aqua blue tiles of the pool gleamed under the harsh rays of the sun as the water moved gently across the length of the pool. Trickling water was like music to my ears as the waterfall feature of the pool oozed into the water below. A couple of my other friends lounged around the area casually. Alexa was stretched out on a sun lounger with a scarlet bikini on, her diamond belly button ring glistening in the sun whilst Fizzy stood chatting to Chad as she threw the last pool float in, clad in a bright pink swimming costume. Bridget appeared to be deep in conversation with Adrian in a black swimming costume, slits across the sides revealing her pale skin. It was the typical party that Fizzy and I had hosted for years, just close friends to mark the end of summer.

One for Sorrow

"It's beautiful out here," Damon complemented, "The weather seemed to know what was going on today."
"Yeah," I replied, "It's the best I've seen it in Eastmere for a while. Make yourself at home. I'll be back in a minute."

Damon nodded his head with a smile before approaching a sun lounger, removing his shirt in one swift movement before stretching out next to Alexa. She raised her sunglasses, shrugged her shoulders before returning to the soaking up the rays of the suns.
"Is this where the party's at?" Andy Fisher asked as he strolled in, clearly letting himself in.
"Babe," Alexa grinned as she stood up and strutted towards him.
"Damn it!" I heard Fizzy cry out, "Could have sworn it was going to be Ian. I'll go get my purse."
Bridget just smirked from where she stood with Adrian and I shook my head. I looked around at my friends around me and the people that I had surrounded myself with, gleaming softly. Somehow I knew despite the secrets that seemingly existed, it would be an enjoyable day.

"You okay now?" I questioned Adrian as I approached him at his locker.

His eyes flew to mine as if he was shocked but softened when he saw that it was me who had spoken. I gave him a small smile to show I wasn't asking him anything bad, just wanted to know if he was okay. The next week of school had rolled towards us all a bit too quickly. Yesterday was drab in comparison to the pool

party atmosphere that existed Saturday. Both Fizzy and I were gleaming from ear to ear as guests complimented us on a successful party. Now, the thought of school just seemed to put a downer on our party mood.
"Yes," he gave me a grim smile, "Thanks for asking."
I nodded, my own smile filling my lips, "What happened anyway?"
"Er- just a bad hamburger, I suspect," he smiled as if he was proud of himself. I could recall him still looking frazzled at the pool party on Saturday. It was strange to see him like that. Adrian was usually so collected but he seemed to be a mess for the entire afternoon. I tried to get a chance to speak to Adrian but it was hard in between his and Bridget's frequent conversations.
"Ooh, I wouldn't eat there again then," Bridget commented, coming up beside me, interlinking her arm with mine, "My mom made us cookies again."
    She reached into her bag and passed me one. The warmth from the cookie radiated across my fingers, spreading a smile across my face.
"Don't you want one Adrian?" I gestured for Bridget to pass him one.
"He's allergic to wheat," Bridget said quietly.
"I still feel ill anyway," Adrian interrupted, sharing a look with Bridget.
"Okay," I frowned, shrugging it off.
    I took a huge bite of the cookie as I let the warmth of it fill me. A smile grew on my lips and Bridget just shook her head at me, she knew how much I loved them cookies. I knew there was something

going on between Bridget and Adrian but I couldn't decipher what. Fizzy's question from earlier in the weekend didn't reveal anything new. I used to think they were in a secret relationship but I couldn't think of any reason why they would hide it. In school, there were a fair handful of people who liked Bridget, a couple of which I could admit to being jealous of before Damon came along. The same was for Adrian as well. He cast aside much female attention he received, I mean it's not like Alexa hid her quest for him.

  However, they were always exchanging looks of secret messages with their eyes. Bridget had said when Adrian first showed up that they were distant family friends. I thought they were just old friends but it seemed like more than that, almost as if they shared a mutual trait or interest that nobody else did. Adrian and Bridget's relationship was completely baffling.
"Are you coming to Mag's pie place after school?" I asked Bridget.
"Erm, no. I have some of my history essay to finish," she lied.

  Her eyes flickered suddenly which added to my evidence that she was lying, I knew we wrote our essays together a week ago, when we first got given it.
"And I have some work to catch up on from the lessons I missed when I was ill," Adrian excused.

  His eyes flashed to Bridget's again then moved back to mine. They both seemed uneasy through both probably lying but I let it slide.
"Come on, we've got to get to English," Bridget gave a tug on my arm and readjusted her bag.

"See you soon," I waved to Adrian who smiled before turning to leave.
"So, English. Why are we doing English if we're American?" Bridget seemed puzzled.
"I don't have the answer. Ask Mr Franks," I said, exasperated with a roll of my eyes and Bridget just laughed at me, I joined in playfully.

The rest of the day passed by and I kept a close eye on Adrian and Bridget. There is definitely something going on with them but Bridget doesn't keep secrets from me. I analysed everything I knew in my head about Adrian's history and how that linked to Bridget but it became apparent that I did not know a lot. Adrian was my friend but he was a mystery, he kept his private life well hidden, almost as if his existence was a big secret.
"Alina!"

I whipped around to reveal Alexa who brought me out of my thoughts, running up to catch me and I frowned. It wasn't often she addressed me in the school corridors unless it was about cheer practise. Alexa was another mystery to me, ever since the beginning of summer between freshman year and sophomore year for Alexa, she changed into someone I didn't recognise anymore. She always used to come around and hang with Fizzy and I but she suddenly changed. Her skirts got shorter, her neckline plunged and she was very self-assured, more than she used to be anyway. She always seemed to be surrounded by people, guys who wanted to be with her and girls who wanted to be her but yet she always seemed so lonely. Sometimes I wondered why she chose that life for herself but it wasn't my place to turn her back into the wholesome cousin we grew up with.

"Is there anything going on between Bridget and Adrian?" she enquired, a sultry smile forming on her lips as a male admirer passed by

I pondered on what to say for a couple of seconds, knowing what Alexa truly wanted. It was no secret that Alexa had wanted Adrian as soon as he arrived at school. He was the only male that hadn't fallen head over heels for her. The fact that someone like Bridget got there first just fuelled her fire. But Adrian didn't want her, and Alexa couldn't understand that.

"I'm unsure," I stated simply, "If they were an item than I would probably be the first one to know."

"Thanks Alina, you will keep me updated, won't you," her face changed to a pleading one and I gave her a sharp nod, "Thank you."

She strutted away and it felt as if I had made a huge mistake. Alexa isn't that nice unless she wants something.

"Since when was Alexa that friendly with you?" Bridget asked as both she and Adrian came up beside me.

They were stood a reasonable distance apart and Adrian had a stern look on his face, almost contorted in pain. I was about to enquire when Bridget's mom pipped her horn. Both bid me goodbye and I paused in confusion. I watched Bridget climb into her Mom's car with a final wave. I hoped she was okay.

One for Sorrow

When I turned to look for Adrian, I realised he was already gone. I frowned; I hadn't seen a car pull up and I knew he didn't use public transport. My eyes scanned the parking lot for any sign of him, but there was none. I sighed and instead looked around for Fizzy. She had just walked out of the school and walked up to meet me as she struggled with her violin case. A grin of joy crossed her facial features as she stood next to me.

"Are you okay?" she asked, as we began to walk out of the school grounds.

"Yeah, it's been a long day," I sighed, "Do you think there's anything going on between Adrian and Bridget?"

Fizzy looked at me almost quizzically and then looked at her feet.

"No, I think they have a shared secret but I don't think they're dating," she answered honestly.

"I'm not sure to be honest, they seem to be sneaking around a lot," I added and she nodded.

"Maybe, they're dating," she suggested and I shrugged.

It wasn't really my business, though Alexa seemed to have made it my business. The only thing I knew for sure was that they were both hiding something, they had been since Adrian arrived back in Eastmere.

Chapter Eight- Adrian

I had gone back to the old house I had been staying in. It had been empty for years; I knew because it had been empty the last time I visited in the eighties. The country style kitchen was dark when I entered. I rolled my shoulders before moving to the cupboard and drawing out the matchbox. I lit some of the candles and the hand-held gas lamp that I had left on the cold kitchen counter. My eyes found a blue cool bag on the kitchen counter, Bridget had been here. I pulled the zip of the bag open to find my usual supply of blood bags. Effortlessly, I stacked them in the refrigerator, stocking the means of my survival back up. I made a mental reminder to thank Bridget for the delivery when I next saw her. The task had reminded that my demon was burning in the back of my throat; I needed blood.

I unlocked the door to the basement, careful not to rattle the keys too much. The soft scrape of the door against the concrete made me shiver. I descended the cellar steps gracefully, lighting another candle downstairs. My eyes glanced around, making sure that everything was still where it should be. I gently pulled the fridge door open, careful not to pull it off its hinges. A sigh left my lips as my hand grabbed a bag of O negative, chucking it into the pan. I watched it until the metallic smell of blood lingered in the air and brought it off heat. The scorching burn in my throat was almost eating me alive, I did not care if it was not warm enough yet, I needed it. Grasping the cup, I threw my head back, pouring the burning liquid down my throat as it quenched the thirst.

Another sigh left my lips. I took another bag, repeating the process, and taking sips of the liquid. I slumped against the hard-concrete wall and I began to feel sluggish. Images flashed in my mind like a kaleidoscope of colour and an attempt to blink them away failed. Before I knew it, I lost sense of all my surroundings completely and my eye sight was not clear. No longer was I in a dark damp basement, I was now being blinded by the fluorescent sting of the lights.

***

"Harry!" Alexa's sultry voice called as she walked down the corridor, swaying her hips seductively. "Alexa," Harrison drawled, walking out of the room, to my distress wearing nothing, completely naked.

I wondered where his dignity had gone, I watched the memory curiously. I could tell that she was using her allure; Harrison's mind was fogged with lust.
"Is this all for me?" she almost purred and I had a feeling that she was referring to his nudity.

My face contorted into one that showed disgust. I glanced around alarmed, wondering why I was seeing what I was seeing. I could not understand what the purpose of this was and why I was seeing Alexa and Harrison.

"Maybe," he attempted to tease with her but his eyes failed him as they trailed longingly down her body.

A sultry smile filled her lips and she placed her bag in the corner. Gently, she placed a finger on his chest and drew it down his torso, Harrison sucking in a deep breath along the way. Teasingly, she shed her leather jacket, dumping it on the floor without another thought. Her brown orbs met Harrison's as she took her black shoes off and she played with her hem line on her shirt.

"Come on babe," he reasoned, a croak breaking in his voice.

"In time," she giggled.

I wanted to look away but something about the scene enticed me to continue watching. Alexa was posing a concept very unusual to me.

In one slow and painful movement, her shirt was off and a groan left his lips. Harrison walked forward but she took a step back, landing in the rays of the sunlight that seeped through the blinds. It highlighted her tanned skin, making it glow and the jewel that hung from her belly button glisten.

"You wore my favourite colour," he murmured, referring to the crimson colour of her bra and Alexa grinned triumphantly.

Harrison's hands rested on the curves of Alexa's hips as his eyes bored into Alexa's. A twinkle was evident in Alexa's eyes and she appeared to be happy, which is something Alexa did not feel often. I could feel her loneliness as I could feel my own, it was something that consumed the both of us. Her lips pressed gently to Harrison's and he deepened it immediately, pulling Alexa against his bare skin. "Hello!" I called out but no-one answered.

I shut my eyes tight, I could not watch this anymore. My hands flew to my ears, making sure I could not hear anything either and waited, still clueless about why I was seeing what I was seeing.

***

I was not sure how long I was unconscious for but I woke up against the cool concrete behind me. It took a couple of minutes to adjust to my surroundings, leaving me feeling vulnerable. Carefully, I eased myself up, leaving half of the blood in my flask. A wave of nausea flooded me and it felt as if someone had beheaded me. I blinked a couple of times as I gained my focus back. I felt a pounding sensation in my head, something that was completely unfamiliar to me. A ringing filled my ears as the numbness in my body left.
"Ah," I mumbled before moving quickly to my jacket which I left hanging over the side of the counter.

The image of Alexa and Harrison burned bright in the back of my mind. A sudden loud chiming noise startled me. I hissed at the darkness, my canines dropping down into place.

I looked around with wide eyes and listened, but the only thing I could hear were birds chattering outside and a dear calling. I reached into a back pocket and drew out the small metal device shuddering in my hand.

"Slide the lock to the green side," Bridget's voice echoed in my mind.

I followed her orders and brought the device to my ear as Bridget's voice called to me. My attention darted back as the volume of Bridget's voice startled me, I was not used to hearing her that loud.

"Adrian," she spoke into her own device.

"Hello," I greeted and a small sigh left her lips.

"So, you figured it out?" she laughed at my lack of knowledge regarding modern day technology and before I could answer, she continued, "Have you looked at the book of shadows yet?"

My eyes flickered to the book resting on the table in the basement. The corners of the battered book were curled up and the pages a yellow weathered colour. It felt as if a presence passed through me, a shiver passing down my spine. I noticed that it was happening more often in the recent days.

"No, I am very wary about what the book will reveal," I expressed and she sighed again.

"I know Adrian but I don't think we have a choice anymore," she pointed out and I nodded in agreement, "A lot of strange things have been going on. That book was open to a page when you found it and Anna's cave has been untouched since the night she was burnt, that page must have something important on it. The town almost seems to be getting stronger. Do you feel it?"

"Yes, I do," I agreed and she was silent for a couple of seconds, "I will talk to you tomorrow."

One for Sorrow

"Bye Adrian," she hung up before I could even manage to remove the device from my ear.

A sigh left my own lips. My eyes found The Book of Shadows again and I could not seem to remove my attention. Alexa's memory seemed to fill my mind but I pondered on why I witnessed it. I was unsure on why I saw what I had and what I was supposed to do with that information. I felt like I needed to speak to Alexa about what I saw. There was a lot that I misunderstood about her, a lot that many people misunderstood about her. It was almost like she was the modern-day version of Anna, people believed she would live up to her stereotype. The town thought Anna was dangerous because of what she was, everyone thinks Alexa's just interested in sleeping around. I knew her habits were more than just habits, I knew she did what she did for a reason, Alexa did everything with a purpose.

I slumped onto the stool and heaved a long sigh. Nothing made sense in Eastmere.

***

The halls emptied quickly when the shrill sound of the bell sounded and I stared down the white walls, almost as if I needed to do something. The sound of plastic scraping against concrete floor reached my ears and my eyes looked at the closet. Cautiously, I walked forward and silently pushed down the handle to discover it was unlocked. There was a sudden movement on the other side so I forced the door open. "What-"

One for Sorrow

Mr Ford cut himself off when he realised what I had just witnessed. He had Alexa pushed up against the wall and her skirt had ridden up to around her waist. The two of them looked at me with their lips red and swollen, there was no mistaking what was going on. Alexa's eyes flashed with concern for a moment before they narrowed into hardened slits, almost sharp enough to kill someone with.
Instead of turning to me like I expected, Mr Ford started on Alexa, "This is your fault!"
Alexa's expression changed into a smirk before answering. He should have known that he could not shake Alexa. She had a way forward for everything and everyone, "Try telling that to the principle."

Alexa pushed him away and stood up straight, pulling her skirt down to cover the necessities. She crossed her arms over her chest, Mr Ford's eyes glancing down before he gulped. Mr Ford's mouth then gaped open for a couple of seconds before he closed it, coming up with a defence strategy.
"You seduced me!" he cried out as he struggled to speak.
"Try telling that to the principle," she repeated again and a cruel laugh left her lips, "I'm the sweet innocent girl in this situation."
"You best not go to the principle," his eyes narrowed at me and I shrugged.
"Maybe you should have thought about that before you enticed a student," I ended the conversation and followed Alexa out of the door.

She did not stop to see what I was going to do with the information that I had just seen. She strutted

along the floor, her heels clicking behind her until I turned her around to face me. Her eyes glared at me but softened to their usual harshness when she realised that I meant no harm. I opened my mouth to speak but I was clueless regarding what to say, I did not even know where to begin. Her eyes rolled before she started the conversation off, I should have known she would not hang around to hear what I had to say.
"What Adrian, I need to go find someone to finish my business off," she looked at her perfectly manicured nails.
"Why him?" I asked.
"I get bored easily with the guys in this school," she said.
"Why do you sleep around at all? Why label yourself like that?" I questioned and she shook her head.
"It doesn't matter Adrian," and she walked away.

One minute she was trying to get close to me, the next she was cold towards me. There was something going on with Alexa and I needed to know what, it might have something to do with the curse. Before I could go after, Alina stood beside me as she watched her cousin walk away.
"Are you okay Adrian?" Alina stood beside me, her backpack dangling from one shoulder.
"Yes, I am okay," I offered a meek smile and she nodded her head.
"I just wanted to check on you, you seem quiet," she stood beside me with a sceptical look in her eyes.
"I am always quiet," I pointed out almost playfully.
"More than usual," she shook her head with a small laugh.

"It is just a hard time of year," I excused myself.
"Anniversary?" She guessed.
"I know it was a long time ago but it's still hard," I admitted.
"I'm here if you ever need me," Alina wrapped her arms around my neck and I hung mine loosely around her waist.

I appreciated the gesture but there was nothing she could do for me. I was alone and I would always be alone. However, she would never understand that. Alina had surrounded herself with a large group of people, almost a community and she had her sister and a few other close friends she could rely upon. I rely upon Bridget for my motivation in this world because there is no-one else for me. Nobody else could ever know the truth of what I am. I choose to be alone as it gives me a sense of security, if they knew, it would not be a choice anymore and then I would truly be alone. Alina and her sister were as close as two sisters could be and I admired the comfort they must get from each other knowing they had a best friend in the form of a sister.
"What did Alexa want?" Alina questioned.
"What she usually wants," I laughed lightly to try and be less solemn.
"Sounds about right. Come on, Bridget and I are meeting up for pizza, you can come with us if you would like?" Alina suggested.
"No, I am okay," I shook my head.
"I insist," she demanded, taking my hand, "Come on, Bridget's in the car park waiting for us."

One for Sorrow

I followed Alina out of the carpark, spying Bridget in her car almost immediately. She gave me a look of question within her eyes and I just gave a bit of shrug. I followed Alina out of politeness, to make her feel better about herself, this lunchtime meeting had nothing to do with me. My feelings would never change, I will never become attached to anyone anymore, it is safer to be alone.

Chapter Nine- Alina

"It was in the 1700s, after the period that was later known as the 'witch burning decade', the forefathers made a plight to banish all suspected witches in Eastmere instead of burning them because-" Mr Geoffries paused in his lecture, "Is something wrong Mr Trent?"

    Mr Geoffries looked at Damon with a raised eyebrow, expectantly waiting for an answer. I knew why he was annoyed. I had been sat next to Damon for the whole last hour and I'll admit that neither of us had written a word because we were too busy making puppy eyes at each other. His eyes were just so dreamy, I was too captivated. I could not understand what I was feeling for Damon, I had never felt like this with anyone before. It was incomprehensible to me why I felt like that. There was something about Damon pulling me to him and I was unsure what it was or why that was happening. The first rule of Mr Geoffries class was to pay attention and that was something both me and Damon were failing completely at.

"No sir," Damon said, shaking his head adamantly, "Sorry."

"Can you tell me in what year the forefathers made their plight?" Mr Geoffries had walked closer towards us, hands on his hips and a smirk on his lips. He knew that neither of us were paying attention.

"1700," Alexa muttered from behind us, flicking her hair behind her shoulder before returning to stare at her perfectly manicured nails.

"1700," Damon answered, catching the teacher out.

"Er yes, well done Mr Trent," Mr Geoffries frowned, before turning to me, "So Alina, why did the forefathers begin to banish suspected witches instead of burning them?"

"Because they killed over a hundred girls and the men outnumbered them almost three to one by 1710," I answered, not taking my eyes from Damon.

"Right," Mr Geoffries moved back to the front of the class.

"I was wondering," I paused to lick my lips nervously as I felt the rush of blood start to tickle my ears pink, "Do you want to come over tonight? We're having Mom's burnin' pig pulled pork."

I smiled at him hopefully as I looked at him through my lashes. I saw him shuffle nervously in his seat before he opened his mouth to speak. I struggled to breath as I waited in anticipation for him to answer me, it was almost suffocating me.

"Well, burnin' pig does sound tempting," he grinned, "Is it hot?"

"It has a kick," I smirked, giggling slightly.

My Mom's spicy pork could blow even the most experienced chilli-eaters heads off if they didn't know the secret. I had begged Mom to make it this morning since it's her afternoon off because I desperately wanted to invite Damon over. Mom just shook her head at me with a small smile, knowing how love-struck I was and agreed, especially since Dad was on a late tonight and would only be home for a couple of hours. Damon and I had only known each other for just under two weeks, but I couldn't wrap my head around the way he made me feel. There was something about him. It was almost as if fate wanted us to be together, as if it was written in stone hundreds of years ago that Damon and I would connect in the way we had, and be partners in the way we were becoming. I had to get to know him better and this was one of the best ways of doing it. I felt a small smile fill my lips as he turned back towards me, an answer hanging on the tip of his tongue.

"Well, in which case, I accept your invitation," Damon said.

"Be at mine for seven," I instructed.

Suddenly, the bell rang, startling us out of our trance. I quickly grabbed my stuff and made my way towards the door, grouping with the rest of my classmates.

"Hey!" Damon called, scrambling to catch up to me and placing a hand on my arm, "I don't know how to get to where you live. Chad brought me in the weekend before and he's at band tonight so I can't get him to drop me off either."

"Well then, you better figure out or find out," I laughed manically to tease him.

"But-" I had already left him, cutting him off from what he was saying.

I felt myself smirk. I wasn't usually this rude to guys I just met but Damon's look of cluelessness that

One for Sorrow

had spread across his face, the same one he wore during English class was just too cute to resist. A dreamy sigh left my lips as I arrived at my locker, turning the lock with the right combination before it swung up.
"Hey sis," Fizzy greeted me and I smiled.
    The words I were about to say were trapped by the sight of Adrian and Alexa talking ahead. A tired look was plastered over Alexa's face, an expression showing through layers of make-up. Adrian however, had a look of curiosity on his face and this completely confused me. Adrian had never looked at Alexa like that and for once Alexa wasn't bothered by Adrian wanting to talk to her, in fact, it looked as if she wanted him to leave. Bridget appeared beside me and looked to where I was staring.
"For once it seems that Alexa is the one bored with Adrian, not the other way around," I laughed in disbelief with a shake of my head.
"Any idea why he would be speaking to her?" Fizzy frowned, taking a step forward in obvious disbelief.
    Bridget remained silent behind me though I could tell that she was burning from the inside, it was almost as if smoke was coming from her ears. Adrian was in trouble, I could tell by her silent anger. Behind me, Bridget pushed past, forcing her way through the swarming mass of students in the corridor frantically pushing their way to their lockers for next lesson. But then, something changed, like the atmosphere had been charged with electricity as Bridget stormed through the swarm. The electricity in the air crackled, causing the hairs on the back of my neck to stand on end. All noise

in the entire building seemed to cease. Everyone in the corridor moved, parted like the red sea as if Bridget was God and Bridget alone controlled the students.

Fizzy squirmed, walking backwards into my shoulder and turned away, a tear slipping down her cheek. Just as Bridget reached Adrian and Alexa, all the usual sounds of school rushed back into the room in a wave, like a sea surge. As everyone seemed to move back to normal, Adrian, Alexa, and Bridget had disappeared. Fizzy and I just looked at each other, she wiped the tear that had escaped out of the corner of my eye like one had her own. Neither of us were sad, just the overwhelming feeling of a surge of emotions had caused tears to pool and eventually fall from our eyes. We just stood there clueless, completely frazzled. "What the hell was that?" Fizzy whispered, her voice cracked as she adjusted to the change of atmosphere. "Eastmere," I replied simply.

Fizzy shook her head and rolled her shoulders, I could see the conflict in her eyes, there was something she wasn't telling me. Before I could press her further, she grabbed a couple of books from her locker and made her way towards the exit across the field. Eastmere just seemed to have proven how powerfully strange it truly was.

***

(Adrian)

"Shit Bridget! What the hell was that?" Alexa looked around, completely confused, her eyes flashing yellow, "I hate faerie magic."

"What the hell is going on?" Bridget demanded, turning to me, "Adrian?"

Her eyes were their natural pure solid purple, which was something very bad. I knew why Bridget was angered by me but I could not tell her the reason I needed to speak with Alexa, if she knew I was having visions then she would blame the curse. I was too afraid to question why I was having visions, I feared I already knew the answer.

"Adrian?" Alexa shrieked, turning on Bridget, "You're the fey that brought us here, wherever we are."

She paused, turning around to scan the area. Her nostrils flared as she took in the scents, her eyes yellow to unleash her true self to intensify her abilities. I did not know myself where we were, so I tipped my head upwards to scent the air. It smelled of mould and mildew, but fresh, a light breeze ruffled the girl's long hair. The stench of the manticore lingered in the air.

"Where are we?" Alexa demanded, turning on Bridget again, "I can smell manticore and it's making me want to hurl."

Hey eyes were still a vivid shade of yellow and her body trembled.

"We're in Anna's cave, now shut up," Bridget snapped.

"Anna's cave? As in, the witch Anna? The reason my family is freaking cursed?" Alexa shrieked, her voice rising with each syllable, "Oh no…"

The energy in the air changed again, focusing around Alexa. She dropped to the ground in a crouch, biting her bottom lip so hard, dark red blood dripped

down on the ground. She shivered; her other form pushing through her human one.
"We don't have time for this Alexa- "Bridget warned as the energy around them both intensified.

My monster picked up at the excitement, forcing its own way out. My teeth punctured my tongue; a thin trickle of blood filled my mouth. It had to get out.
"Adrian," Bridget grabbed my arm so suddenly, I turned on her, hissing savagely with my teeth bared at their maximum.

In the commotion, a low growl rippled from the ground as Alexa rose on four paws. The shadow of the manticore crept from one of the deeper tunnels. My body froze rigidly as the creature moved past the hollow gap in the cave wall.
"What do we do?" Bridget whispered.
"Why did you bring us here?" I shook my head.

Alexa released a low predatory growl, deep in her throat. It made me whimper mentally and recoil in fear. Her aura demanded respect, she was alpha. Bridget watched her wearily as Alexa backed up. The air seemingly calmed as we all anticipated Alexa's next move.
"Adrian," Bridget breathed but before she could continue, Alexa had pounced.

A roar echoed from the stone walls, a battle cry almost as the manticore launched himself towards Alexa. But it was no match for Alexa's rage as she latched onto him. For a while, it was hard to tell who was winning as they tumbled and shoved each other against the wall. A groan of pain was audible as it paused in its track. Its eyes rolled in unconsciousness as it lost its grasp on the world before it sank to the ground, defeated.

"I-"

Alexa cut Bridget off as she released a whine. I walked forward to try and help her. Blood matted her fur in places but it was hard to tell if it was her blood or her victims. The manticore's body lay still and seemed to fade into nothingness. I had heard somewhere that a manticore could not be properly, permanently killed, but it was killed for now. Alexa released another groan as she shifted back to her human form. Bridget stepped forward to help Alexa but her eyes shot a warning glare, telling Bridget to stay away. She wobbled for a minute as she stood on her human legs but soon enough stood up straight. I looked away to show her some privacy until she could cover herself. A hiss of pain slipped out of her mouth and she turned to observe a deep gash. The metallic smell of blood hit me at once and I shrunk into the far corner, almost in disgust.

"Let me help you," Bridget offered but Alexa scowled at her.

"Like I said earlier, I don't want your faerie magic," she spat out, venom latched onto her voice, "I do want your jacket though."

Bridget shrugged off my long jacket that she had borrowed for the day like she usually did. She handed it over to Alexa who snatched it from her grasp, slipping her arms through the sleeves and zipping it up. She pulled a face at the scent of the jacket, smelling me on it before turning towards me.

"You owe me Adrian."

Our eyes glanced to the beast before returning to each other. Alexa brushed the dirt from the jacket. "And-"
Bridget cut me off, "If you don't want my magic then find your own way out of here."

She whispered something in a slippery tone and vanished before our eyes. Alexa and I just looked towards each other, our eyes seemingly staring each other down. It appeared as if Alexa wanted to say something to me, almost as if she wanted to release the burdens she carried onto me but she failed to say anything. She was like me in many ways, alone through choice even though she's surrounded by people.
"I will pay you back, I will watch your back," I suggested, "Try to keep you safe."
"It's pretty clear that I don't need your help," she flicked her hair behind her shoulder.
"I-" Before I could finish my sentence, Bridget had brought me back to her side, a dangerous look in her eyes.

It alarmed me how strong her magic was considering her age, and what blood line she descended from. The amount of darker energy surging through her form was too high. She looked at me expectantly, as if I was supposed to say something but I did not say a word. Bridget rolled her eyes like Alexa usually does before turning to walk towards the open door.
"Don't even bother, I'm going home," she announced and before I could protest, she had disappeared again.

One for Sorrow

I was in the school building, in an English Literature room on the second floor. The dark night poured through the windows. The night was calm outside, but inside, my monster was still awoken and restless, unsated by the calming energy Bridget had inserted into me. My fangs still hung prominently from my upper lip. I ran my tongue along them and tasted a drop of venom on my tongue. It was vile but made the demon more insistent. I wanted to empty the contents of my stomach onto the ground but my body was not able to do that. My mind fought the urges of the monster but it was pointless to resist, I was at the mercy of my inner demon. I moved to the window and unlatched the window lock, before slipping silently into the night. The monster was on the hunt, and I was trapped in a cage, unable to contain it.

Chapter Ten- Alina

Damon was late; it was ten minutes past seven and he still hadn't arrived. I was hovering around the dining table, to the kitchen to check on Mom and Fizzy's cooking then to Dad in the front room, the TV flickering in front of him from across the room. My heart was hammering in my chest like a hummingbird and I could feel my breath coming out in fast, short pants. The nerves were starting to get to me, I knew I was being silly, it was just Damon but that was the point exactly, it was Damon.
"Calm down, Al," he muttered.
"Maybe it would have helped if you told him directions to where we lived instead of telling him to quote 'you better find out' unquote," Fizzy said in a sing-song from the doorway, a tea towel slung over her shoulder. I rolled my eyes at her and huffed, folding my arms across my chest. I knew I was being dramatic but I didn't know what to do or to feel.
"Is this true?" my dad cast me a disbelieving look and sighed, shaking his head. I could hear the amusement in his voice though, my dad was always like that.
    Fizzy began giggling as she walked back into the kitchen and I wanted to wrap my two hands around her neck; she was not helping at all.

One for Sorrow

"Nearly ready," My mother called from the kitchen and my eyes widened in worry as I glanced at the clock hung on the wall.
"I hope he has a good excuse," my dad muttered and I ran my hands through my hair anxiously.
"He does, he didn't know where we lived," Fizzy laughed from the kitchen and I rolled my eyes.
"She has a point," Dad shook his head at me again.
"It sounded good when I said it, I thought it would make him laugh!" I announced, exasperated.
"Well, it's definitely given me a chuckle," Dad shook his head at me with laugh.

    I rolled my eye and flopped onto the sofa. A huff left my lips as I folded my arms over my chest and I could see Dad watching me from the corner of his eyes. I knew the kind of comment he wanted to make, saying that I was more entertaining than the entertainment column of the newspaper but I think he sensed it was dangerous territory as it was. That was the last thing I needed to hear, even if he did mean it as a joke.

    The doorbell chimed and I shot up from my seat, nearly stumbling over in the process and opened the door. My mouth slowly crept down and Damon shot me a sheepish smile. For some reason, I had doubts that he was even coming. I blinked a couple of times just to make sure that he was still there and I hadn't imagined his figure. He was dressed in black dress pants paired with a light blue button-down shirt. I couldn't help but admire how good he looked. Then I remembered my family waiting for him and I felt sick all over again, not sure I was ready for food at all. The fog rolled through the front garden as night invaded Eastmere and I shuddered at the thought of Damon walking here in the dark. I made a mental note to ask Mom to drop him off at the end of the night if he didn't have a lift. The one boy I actually felt close with definitely didn't need disappearing in the night.

"Hey, sorry I'm late. I had to find out from Bridget where you lived," he explained, "Chad's directions were shocking."

"Are you going to let him in?" Fizzy questioned, popping up next to me.

"Shove off," I hissed at her and stood aside, "He's barely been here for a minute, I was just getting to that part."

"And who's fault is that? You should have told him where you lived," Fizzy laughed, "You're letting in the cold, now come on!"

Damon shot me another smile and stepped past me, a wave of cologne hitting me and my own smile graced my lips. He stood hopelessly in the doorway and I shook my head at him as I closed the spookiness of the town behind me. Fizzy giggled joyfully before bounding into the kitchen back to Mom.

"So, you live in a massive old house on the outskirts of town, surrounded by forest and hidden from the main road?" Damon asked.

"Did you not notice when Chad brought you in for the pool party a couple of weeks ago?" I laughed.

"Not really, he talks a lot, I was kind of focused on what he was saying," Damon admitted.

"Well the house is haunted too," I added with a teasing smile.

"Spooky," Fizzy giggled, popping up again.
"I thought you were cooking," I said, annoyed.
"I was, but now food is served. We're waiting for you," Fizzy explained.

    I groaned inwardly then covered it with a smile before taking Damon's hand and leading him to the dining room. The food was all laid out with the smoking pig roast in prime position surrounded by roasted vegetables. My mouth watered almost instantly and I seated next to the head of the table, Damon sitting between both me and Fizzy. A proud, broad grin adorned my mother's face at the feast she had produced. Without a word, she gestured to the food and I was first to attack the boar.

"Slow down Alina," my Dad scolded, picking up his plate mom had already prepared for him, "Guests first."
"Dogs first," I replied, chucking a bit of meat onto the floor which Damon laughed at, making my insides go all gooey.

    Sunny attacked the patterned rug as she devoured the tough skin, releasing a small growl. Damon appeared to be overwhelmed about the amount of food presented and my eyebrows furrowed slightly in confusion.
"What's wrong?" I hissed in a whisper.
"I'm a vegetarian," he replied quietly and I almost spit my pork out all over the table in front of me.
"Well burning pig does sound tempting was your exact words," I spoke out, almost exasperatedly.
"I didn't think you were actually inviting me," he explained and I shook my head with a small smile.

"It doesn't matter, we have home-made potato salad," my mom interrupted, handing over the bowl.
"It's probably because he got lost in your eyes," Fizzy laughed.

I really wanted to kill her right now but before any words could escape my mouth, Mom had begun talking to Damon. Damon smirked at Fizzy's comment and I filled my plate to hide the red that was creeping up my neck and onto my cheeks. Dad placed his coat over his arm before turning his attention to his youngest daughter's words.
"What was that Felicity?" he enquired, "I don't want to hear anything like that, especially about my darling daughter."

Damon's eyes found mine and he flashed me an emotion that was unrecognisable. I rose from my seat and pecked my Dad's cheeks, handing him his flask of Brazilian coffee. He kissed Mom and exited the house, the sound of the car soon fading into the distance and my nerves seemed to dissipate with it. We all began eating again and Damon gave me inconspicuous looks until all four plates were emptied. I released a long sigh of contentment, placing my hands on my stomach.
"That was delicious Mrs Harrington," Damon complemented which put a smile on my lips as well as my Mom's.
"Well thank you Damon, that was very kind of you to say," she blushed slightly, taking the empty plates away.
"Oh, let me help you with that," he rushed up, leading the way out of the room.

Fizzy smirked at me and I shook my head, "What?"
"You are so in love," she giggled, twirling her hair, almost mockingly at me.
"Am not," I argued.
"Are to," she laughed again.
"Am not."
"Are to."

Fizzy pushed her chair back and my hand flew to my mouth before it happened. Damon was carrying through a hot bowl of custard, it quickly falling over as Fizzy pushed her chair into him. It felt as if the room almost fell into complete slow motion, watching as each drop of custard hit my sister.
"I'm so sorry," Damon gushed as he tried to dab the liquid with a napkin to save his embarrassment.
"No, it was my fault," she wiped her forehead, shuddering at the feeling of the liquid running down her spine, "I should have looked first."

Mom gasped as she came in with the apple pie, quickly placing it on the table and moving over to Fizzy, who was frozen to the spot she stood in. It was as if the custard had glued her feet to the carpet.
"Honey, you need to take a cold shower, that's going to scar," Mom demanded, a look of confusion passing over her face at the lack of pain Fizzy was in.

I placed my finger on her arm and licked the liquid to find that it was cold. My lips frowned and Mom's eyebrows furrowed in confusion.
"Cold," I announced, "But delicious."
"I swear my custard was bubbling," she stated.
"It was," Damon confirmed, nodding his head almost a bit too eagerly.

"Oh well, it's too cold now so I'm taking a shower," Fizzy concluded, smiling at Damon before exiting out of the door.
"Well either way Mom, it tasted great," I shrugged.
"Thanks honey," she pecked my cheek delicately.

Damon gave me a sheepish grin and Mom lowered a cloth onto the floor. I scooted back from my chair and crouched down to begin mopping the custard up.
"It's fine, I have carnation milk in the cupboard," she left the room.

Damon gave me another grin as he joined me on the floor to help clear up the mess. This night had been a disaster.

***

"Hey," Bridget smiled as I strolled up the pathway towards Mag's Pie Place, the scent of the honeysuckle plant hitting us in a wave and filling my nose. A content sigh left my lips at the atmosphere I was in. The rays of the autumnal sun caressed my skin gently as the sun beamed through the ivory clouds.
"Hi," I grinned, hooking my arm around hers tightly.

Every second Sunday, Bridget and I made a pact years ago to meet at Mag's Pie Place to catch up whilst we sipped on our favourite drinks. Sometimes I found it nice to talk to her on a one to one basis instead of us being surrounded by our friends. She pushed the door open, the cool air of the aircon hitting me in a wave which I embraced, allowing the door to close behind me. Bridget's hair swayed behind her from her

high ponytail as I followed her to the opposite side of the store where we found the den to be empty; it usually was on a Sunday. She slid into the leather booth on one side and I on the other, placing my bag beside me. Mrs Maguire delivered our usual, two strawberry milkshakes, extra cream with a portion of fresh fries to share. I handed over a twenty-dollar bill, telling her to keep the change since it was my turn to pay. Mrs Maguire smiled before walking away with the note and the tray, leaving the two of us to it. I took a fry, swirling it around in the pink goodness before popping it into my mouth. The sweet contrasted against the saltiness, the usual combination I loved.
"So, how was your dinner with Damon?" Bridget smirked before she took a sip from her frosted glass through the red crazy straw.
"A disaster, he's a vegetarian!" I exclaimed, exasperated.

Some of the students hanging out glared at my outburst and I felt myself recoil in my seat from embarrassment. I felt blood rush up my neck onto my cheeks and I shielded my face with my hair. Bridget just shook her head in amusement before eating a fry. I could tell she was trying to contain her laughter at me but she was failing miserably.
"I don't appreciate that," I scolded playfully, "It was one of the most embarrassing situations I've ever had to sit through."
"Even that time when Blair spilt ice-cream in your hair at your birthday party," Bridget laughed, knowing I would shudder at that memory.
"Yes," I stressed.

"Wow, it must have been bad then. He's a vegetarian? I swear he said yes to your Mom's flaming pork, like you think the word pork would give him a clue it was going to be a meat based meal," Bridget frowned, "It was in history, wasn't it? When you two were making puppy eyes at each other for the whole lesson and annoyed sir."
"That's what I thought," I almost laughed but managed to suppress it, "Then he spilled the custard all over Fizzy. Though she did push her chair into him, it wasn't just that he's clumsy."
"Oh no," her eyes widened, "That must have hurt, is she okay?"
"She's fine, weirdly, it was cold by the time it hit her," I mirrored Bridget's expression from earlier as a frown invaded my features. Bridget seemed to become lost in her thoughts for a short time as she pondered over what I had told her. It wasn't long before she opened her mouth to speak again.
"That is strange," Bridget agreed, "As weird as Eastmere is anyway."
"True," I laughed, "And he walked to mine in the dark, I wished he'd said something if he didn't have a lift."
"At least he got there safe," Bridget shot back.
"I know, don't think he takes my warnings of the town seriously though, probably thinks I'm crazy," I laughed, "Anyway, anything going on with you and Adrian?"
"No, we're just friends. I think he gets lonely sometimes," Bridget revealed and I just nodded my head.
"I see that, he's very reserved," I observed.

"He's been alone for quite a lot of his life so it's what he's used to. People caring for him isn't something he's experienced for a long time. I think he's still trying to adjust to it, I mean he doesn't have any family after all, he's only got his friends to care about him," Bridget expressed her thoughts, twirling the straw around the side of the glass, cream falling into the middle of the glass, "I don't think he's used to having relationships with people. He gets confused on why I stick around? It's sad really, that he's had to live life like that."

"It has only been a year, I guess it is a lot to get used to," I sympathised, "I guess you have to get used to people caring if no-one's ever cared about you. It's kind of sad when you put it like that."

"Yeah, he's getting better though," Bridget nodded her head with her words as she placed another fry in her mouth.

      I felt sorry for Adrian, all my life I had been surrounded by family and friends, Eastmere being like my family but Adrian had never experienced that. I swirled another fry around in my milkshake as I pondered about Adrian and the life that he led. His life had shaped him into something I never thought I would meet, I felt like I needed to help him. I didn't want him to feel alone anymore, I wanted him to know that it was okay to love those around him. I knew Bridget could help me with that, I just needed to try and find a way to get through to him. My eyes wandered over to a magpie sat on the window ledge. It's black beady eyes seemingly glared into my soul, a shiver passing down my spine.

One for Sorrow

"Are you okay?" Bridget frowned at me.
"Yeah, I'll be okay," I gave her a small smile in return.
    Eastmere was getting stranger by the day and I wasn't sure why.

Chapter Eleven- Alina

"Bridget, you did what?" Alexa called out.
"I-"
"You slept with him didn't you," Alexa roared at my best friend, cutting Bridget off from defending herself.
"I'm not a slut like you, that means I didn't sleep with anyone," Bridget replied almost expertly.
"Oh, you call me a slut again and I will," her face reddened and her body trembled in what appeared to be pure anger.
"Or do you want another word for it, how about whore or maybe slag-"

Alexa grasped her raven hair in a large clump, holding Bridget in a head lock. Bridget winced as a strangled cry escaped her lips. She latched onto Alexa's bare tanned legs, clawing at them to try and get her to release her. The air surrounding us cooled dramatically as the wind picked up speed. I found myself swatting my hair out of my face as I tried to get a grasp of the situation.
"Come on girls," I tried to pry them apart with words but Bridget struggled in Alexa's arms.

I grabbed Alexa's arms and her attention flew to me and I stepped back in shock. Her eyes appeared to glow yellow but it soon faded back to her natural brown orbs. I blinked a couple of times, presuming it was a trick of the light. I took a deep breath in, feeling as if I couldn't break the stare that she had held me in before she looked to the ground.

"It's not worth it," she seemed to listen until she landed a square punch on Bridget's jaw.

"Alina," Fizzy's voice filled my ears but the issue in front of me was escalating quickly, requiring my whole attention.

"Not now," I stressed.

"But-" I turned around cutting her off.

"I said not now Felicity," I snapped.

Her features appeared to drop before she turned to walk away, the joy from her face fading immediately. I was going to say something to put her smile back but Bridget released a squeal of pain. She lashed out at Alexa taking a hold of her leg and Alexa released a primal roar. I took Bridget by the waist and attempted to pry her away but it wasn't working, I wasn't strong enough. I felt Alexa's long tanned hands scrape against my back and I let out a squeal of pain. My eyes watered and I took in a deep breath, attempting to supress the pain that had filled me.

"Damon," I called out desperately, my voice hoarse, "Adrian!"

Adrian had me by the waist, pushing me to the side and then held Bridget in his arms, Mack holding Alexa. I lost my balance as my knees buckled, my body falling to the ground with a soft thud. Adrian shot a look to me to check I was alright but was quickly diverted back to Bridget who was struggling to try and escape in his arms. Pain travelled up my arms from the contact and I winced in pain. Damon knelt beside me on the ground, wrapping his arms around me and helping me up. I could feel my heart flutter as he kept his hand on the small of my back. My head felt heavy as I tried to grasp reality. It almost felt as if I had been winded, the energy from the atmosphere drawing on my breath.

"Are you okay?" he asked me to and I nodded, "Are you absolutely sure?"

"Yes, I'm fine thanks," I smiled, taking a breath, "Girls that was completely inappropriate during practise; I'm going to have to suspend you both."

"You can't do that, you're not my captain!" Alexa narrowed her eyes at me.

"I'm sure when I tell Merissa she won't have a problem with it," I shot back, "Just be glad that coach wasn't here otherwise you both would have been off the team."

"Well it's her fault anyway, isn't it," Bridget began, "She shouldn't believe silly rumours. Who did I have sex with anyway?"

"Harry," Alexa replied, checking her hair in the mirror she carried.

"I didn't, why do you care anyway?" I was curious to know myself as Bridget continued, "I've never shown an interest in the guy."

"Well, I don't," she lied, "I just didn't think he'd move on that quickly and to someone like you as well."

"He was trying to make you jealous," Adrian stated the obvious before Bridget could argue back at the snide comment Alexa made, "Creating lies because he hoped it would make you interested in him again, realise you made a mistake."

One for Sorrow

      Alexa looked down with sorrow filling her eyes, something I didn't see her feel often. Alexa lived a life of no regrets, the minute she regretted a decision was the minute she would question her whole being. She lived in the present day, not in the past. Bridget and Alexa walked off with Adrian in tow and I shook my head at them in disbelief.
"Alexa is definitely strange," Damon commented and I nodded in agreement, "Alina."
"Yeah," his eye twinkled nervously, as if he was about to ask me something big.

      I glanced back towards the guys as they walked away slowly, Adrian lingering slightly behind as the two girls talked. Damon cleared his throat and my eyes looked back to his, finding them laced with an emotion he hadn't shown me before.
"Will you go on a date with me?" he asked hopefully, interlacing his fingers with mine.

      I attempted to keep a straight face to tease him but my smile broke through almost instantly. My heart fluttered like a baby bird trying to take flight and I felt the pit of snakes in my stomach squirm.
"Er…" I drawled out, teasing him slightly, "I would love to go out with you Damon."

      He wrapped his arms around me tightly, his heartbeat filled my ears as I rested again his hard chest. I couldn't believe Damon Trent just asked me out. I needed to tell someone, to share my excitement with. Bridget was preoccupied and the only other person I could talk to was Fizzy. I needed to tell Fizzy but then I remembered what I called her. My face dropped in dread as I thought about what I had done to my sister.

Damon pulled away and noticed my reaction straight away, concern lacing his own.
"Are you okay?" Damon asked, worry crossing his eyes.
"Yeah, I will be alright," I nodded my head unconvincingly.

He gave me a pointed look since he knew I was lying, pecked my cheek softly before walking towards the exit of the field. I stood in the middle of the field, alone and exasperated at the thought of what I could do to fix this situation.

***

(Adrian)

"Bitch, do you know how close I was to turning into a wolf just now? How close I was? If I had turned in school…the full moon isn't for another week or so…" Alexa seemed to be on the verge of tears as she sank to a crouch on the football pitch.

Her short skirt and lack of stockings meant there was a lot of skin on show, so I turned away in decency to fix my gaze on Bridget. I could hear Alexa's heavy pants as she tried to calm her breathing to submerge her inner beast. It was obvious that she felt anger, the rage filled her almost to capacity and she was struggling to shift the tsunami that had drowned her.
"You're the one who was spreading the rumour that my best friend had slept with the new guy," Bridget snapped, turning around to place a hand to her

forehead, "And that I was sleeping with Adrian and Harry."

The atmosphere changed as energy began to charge the air surrounding Bridget. As the energy dispersed, I began to feel calmer. Heaving a heavy sigh, Alexa rose to her feet, a glare in her eyes although her demeanour was calm.

"Thanks," she spat at Bridget.

"Look if we're going to figure out this curse, we're going to have to work together," Bridget began, turning to each of us in turn.

"I agree," I said.

"And it wasn't me who started the rumour, you overheard me trying to stop it. I know I don't always see eye to eye with my family but I still like to protect Alina and Fizzy," Alexa admitted.

Bridget nodded her head in understanding, a small smile creeping onto her lips, "I'm willing to call a truce if you are, Alexa. It will benefit us both. I can help you, the next full moon- "

"Don't talk to me about 'moons' faerie," Alexa whipped around to face us both and I saw the flash of her beast.

Her aura ripped a tear in the atmosphere surrounding her, before it settled once again. Hey eyes flashed a bright shade of yellow before the colour dulled into a lightening brown.

"I don't need help; I can look out for myself!"

"Like the time I found you passed out not far from my house," Bridget said, tension brimming on the edge of boiling over, "You were doing just fine then weren't you?"

"I was fourteen. I was scared shitless. Why did I even try to pet that wolf?" she muttered the last question.
"Ladies," I said, interrupting them both.

They both whipped their heads around to look at me, one pair yellow, one pair the colour of a purple midnight sky. I could see the emotion and the passion in both of their eyes.
"Is there a way you could perhaps move past this? Be a little more civilised?" I offered.
"Ha!" Alexa barked out a cruel laugh, "Don't tell me how to be civil, leech."

Alexa turned and spat at the ground. The tang of blood tickled the air. My hand flew to my nose to prevent the temptation releasing the beast. I was unsure whether the blood of a being of the moon would awaken the beast, I was unwilling to take that risk.
"Alexa, don't make this any harder than it is," Bridget warned.
"I am sorry Alexa. I know It is not easy controlling your own personal monster. You and I both know that," I said, hoping to make a truce.
"You're right, it is hard. Which is why I'm leaving," Alexa announced.
"No, you're not, you can't," Bridget interrupted, "We need you, even though I hate to admit it."
"Why would I help you?" Venom dripped from her every word and I did not have an answer for her.

I did not know what I or Bridget even could offer her, the only solution I could come up with to what you could offer a werewolf was a steak.

"Adrian," Bridget warned, knowing what I was thinking before turning to Alexa again, "Have you ever thought that maybe there's a cure."

Alexa's stance shifted and I knew Bridget had hit a soft spot. Alexa eyed her up for a couple of seconds, testing whether she was telling a lie. It was then that I realised that I was no longer part of the equation. This was between the faerie and the werewolf so I slipped off the school's football field and back into the confinements of the school.
"Fizzy, calm down," the sound of a male's voice pleading filled my ears.

My legs quickly carried me to a different part of the school. The smell of bleach filled my nostrils but it was soon dominated by the strong scent of a witch. Thoughts of Anna filled my mind until the elegant blonde waves of Felicity caught my eye.

Silently, I strolled forward to see her being comforted by a boy I did not know the name of. She sunk down the side of the lockers, wrapped in his embrace, his arms were placed on her delicate waist as she shed the tears of her soul. Curiosity quickly filled my mind as I watched the scene unfold before me. The sound of thunder rattled the atmosphere and the heavens opened, releasing its own contents onto us. Felicity's heavy sobs that vibrated her body matched the rhythm of the thunder. Before I could think deeper into the sudden weather change, Felicity's cries turned into quiet breaths and a conversation was about to begin.
"I can't believe she spoke to me like that," she expressed as she wiped her eyes.

One for Sorrow

Mystery man handed her a tissue which she accepted with a gracious smile. Carefully, she dabbed under, cautious to avoid her make-up and looked back to the man, sympathy filling his eyes.
"Reece, do you have any siblings?" He shook his head and she mumbled, "Lucky."

He laughed and re-wrapped his arms around her tighter, she snuggled into his chest,
"But my drummer is like my brother," he expressed, "You know chad, right?"
"Of course, I know Chad silly," I heard Felicity giggled.
"Well I know that," Reece shook his head, "I was just saying his name"
"Chad's great," Fizzy admitted.

***

"From the top Chad!" Reece ordered and he nodded, tying his bandana tighter on his head.

Reece shook his head and laughed before strumming the opening chord to a pop song I was definitely unfamiliar with. I watched as Chad's afro bounced in time to the beat of the drum. Reece's mouth opened as he sang the opening lyric. My hands flew to my ears to protect them as modern music flowed into my ears. I could not understand why I was seeing this. It reminded me of the scene with Alexa and Harrison, it had no relevance to my life at all. My eyes were fixed on Chad as beads of sweat trickled down his face. He was so engrossed in his drumming that he didn't noticed when Felicity entered the room.

Reece's eyes widened in joy at the sight of her and he almost fell from his chair as he moved to talk to her. Chad stopped drumming abruptly and a smile charmed his lips.

I did not know whose blood I had consumed, but I knew it was either Reece or Chad. I did not understand what I was seeing and I was not sure that I wanted to.

"Hey Fizzy," Chad greeted as he slung a blue towel over his shoulder.

"Hey Chad, you okay?" she asked and he nodded.

He was about to ask her something but it was left on the tip of his tongue as Reece stole her attention. It was evident to me that Chad had feelings for Felicity; his eyes twinkled in an emotion that I had seen too many times in my life time; I knew that emotion better than anyone.

"What are you doing today?" Felicity enquired, looking at him as she peered through her layered fringe.

"We have band practise until two and then I'm free, why?" he smiled brightly.

He knew what was coming better than Chad did. The smirk that filled his lips urged Felicity to continue. Chad scratched the back of his neck nervously but covered it with an action like that of wiping sweat. If I had a heart it would be breaking right now for Chad.

"I was wondering if you wanted to hang out," she offered, twirling her hair flirtatiously, "You know, maybe I could play violin with you lot and see how it goes and stuff."

One for Sorrow

Chad's expression dropped into a cold look of despair. He removed himself from the conversation and slumped onto his stool. His hands grasped the oak wood and he softly drummed, listening in on the conversation without the two of them knowing.
"Where?" My attention flew immediately back to Reece who had his own smirk on his lips.
Chad shifted on his seat as he anticipated an answer from Felicity.
"My house," she revealed and Reece's eyes almost widened in happiness.
From the look on Chad's face, I could see all the weird fantasy's that ran through his head. My eyes blinked as I tried to coax myself out of this dream state.
"My Mom and Dad are having a small barbeque; they said I could invite a couple of friends. Alina's inviting Bridget and Adrian," my attention changed again at the sound of my name, "So I'm inviting you, and you too Chad, you're welcome too."
Chad's head flew up, his locks of hair bouncing uncontrollably. Shock was evident on his face but he nodded, possibly a bit too eagerly. I wanted to know why I was watching this. I wanted to know if there was anything to learn from this memory. But most of all, I wanted to know why I was seeing memories, something I had never experienced after being a monster for as long as I could remember.

***

One for Sorrow

"I think she was just a bit stressed, if you talk to her now, she'll probably apologise and beg for your forgiveness, bribing you with those mini chocolates that I know you're addicted to," Reece tried to comfort Felicity as his arm was slung loosely around her petite shoulders.

Felicity released a small giggle as her face filled with joy. Thunder seemed to end with a small rumble. As Felicity's smile grew, sun poured in from one of the windows in the hall. Lockers rattled as someone crashed against it in a rush.
"Why don't you come over to band practice after school?" Reece asked Felicity, taking her chin in one hand whilst the other went around her body, drawing her closer to connect their lips.

It deepened quickly and made me feel as if I were intruding on an intimate moment in their own world where I was not welcome. Yet I still watched. I was fascinated by their sudden fall into love. Their actions reminded me of myself and Anna.

Felicity and Reece were similar to us and were about the same age that I-
The sharp sound of the school bell shocked me out of my stupor, forcing me to crouch into a defensive position like a wild animal forced into a corner by hunters with pitch forks and flaming torches, like Anna was all of them years ago. Breath left me in a hiss, air struggling through my teeth. Classroom doors started slamming open and the corridor erupted into a cacophony of noise, talking, chatting, laughter, screams, wails, sounds.

I recollected myself and pretended that I was tying my shoe laces. Students passed me, oblivious to the monster they were walking by. I stood up and slipped away into the crowd, then back outside. The weather outside had cleared up, the storm from earlier having dissipated into the atmosphere like the end of a play fading to black. It only took me a moment to find my way back to the place where Bridget and Alexa had been finding an agreement. As I arrived, the smell of wolf was strong in the air, musky and fresh.

Alexa's other form met my eyes with her yellow ones and she blinked twice before slipping away into the forest, which provided the perimeter for the back of the school. Bridget smiled when she saw me and wove her way into my arms, her warm hands settling on the small of my back and her head rested against my shoulder.

"I love you," she whispered.

Chapter Twelve- Alina

"Fizzy?" I knocked twice gently on her pink floral and butterfly design bedroom door. I could hear music being played from inside her room and the music paused at my knock.

My sister opened the door, her smile faded at the sight of me and I was certain she was about to slam the door in my face. I suddenly felt nerves fill me, not something I associated when having a conversation with my younger sister.

"Please," I felt my eyes soften as I pleaded with her and she cautiously stepped out of her room, "I'm really sorry, Alexa and Bridget stressed me out and as soon as it had left my mouth, I wanted to take it back."

"You used my full name, Felicity is the name people use when I'm in trouble," she folded her arms dramatically over her chest, "It wasn't my fault they were fighting, it was wrong to take it out on me."

Fizzy wasn't one for holding grudges usually, even when we were little within a couple of hours she would give in and it would be like nothing ever happened. She had always been a forgiving character; it was one of the many reasons why she was so likeable. I knew it wouldn't take long for her to accept my apology but it didn't stop me from trying to win her forgiveness back.

"Please," I begged, guilt consuming me.

She tried to keep a straight face but her smile of elation cracked onto her lips. I wrapped my arms around her as I embraced her in a tight hug. She giggled into my shoulder before she pulled away from me.

"I'm actually kind of glad, Reece spent about ten minutes comforting me," a blush spread across her cheeks, "I have band practise tonight."

"I have a date tonight," I revealed with a grin and her eye widened immediately.

"With whom?" she squealed.

"Damon," my grin grew wider and Fizzy released a shriek of excitement, "I mean, it's only taken like three weeks."

"Girls," Dad appeared on the steps. "What's going on?"

"Alina has a date with Damon, that boy from last Friday," Fizzy opened her mouth and the words had spilled out before she could even think about her revelation.

Fizzy slammed her hands to her mouth dramatically as my eyes narrowed at her. The doorbell interrupted what Dad was about to say and I heard mom's heels against the hallway floor before Mom pulled the door open. All three of us peered down the hallway and down the stairs to see who had arrived. We all listened carefully and waited curiously to see who the visitor was for. The suspense in the air was almost enough to slice with a dagger as we waited to see who was on the other side of the door.

"Hi Damon," she greeted, speaking the name of the last person who needed to be in my Dad's eyesight right now.

I rushed down the stairs before either Dad or Fizzy could squeeze past me to be welcomed by Damon's warm embrace. He just chuckled as he wrapped his arms around me tightly and I snuggled into his hard chest. I sank into him before Sunny made a noise behind me, forcing her way between us.
"Sunny," I scowled, but rubbed her behind her golden ears anyway.

Sunny wagged her tail and leant against Damon's legs, grinning up at him.
"She really is a great looking dog," Damon commented, Sunny yipping and forced her nose into his hand, licking his fingers.
"She likes you," I giggled.
"I like you too, Sunny. I have a dog at home too. Maybe we could walk them together sometime," he suggested.
"I'd like that," I answered as Sunny moved to brush against me, "I think Sunny would too."

I supressed a giggle as Damon grinned at me, his smile causing my insides to go gooey. He held the front door open for me as my Mom had disappeared elsewhere into the house to stop it from closing onto me.
"Thank you, kind sir," I curtsied before a golden mass barged past me and into the cooling air.
"Sunny!" I called, moving to chase after her.
"Hold on, I want to talk to Mr Trent," My Dad's voice held a warning in it and I shuddered from previous

One for Sorrow

memories. Dad was always like this with guys I was associated with, even with Adrian he was like that even though we both made it clear he was just a friend. Dad actually took a liking to Adrian, something about how he had thanked my Dad for looking after his daughters. I think the specific words he used was that Adrian was an honourable man.

Damon's eyes found mine and he visibly gulped, his Adam's apple bobbing nervously before he followed my Dad into the house. It felt like he was going for a death sentence.
"I guess I'll just go collect Sunny," I mumbled as I left to find her from a tree she was jumping up at.

My eyes found Sunny barking at a grey squirrel which was perched neatly on a branch. I shook my head with a small grin. Pulling a treat from my pocket, I tempted her away as her tail wagged in desperation. I managed to pull her away and back into the house with a lot of effort. It was strange, she wasn't usually one for running away, then again, she never could resist a squirrel. Just as I closed the front door, trapping Sunny on the inside, Damon appeared from behind the house.
"Good chat Mr Trent," my Dad called out from the kitchen.
"Yes, Mr Harrington, I'll keep your words in mind, let's go Alina," he hurried down the path. Once again, I shook my head and laughed at Damon's reaction.
"Where are we going?" I asked with a giggle.
"You know the statues script, I figured that there has to be something in the town's history," he explained.
"Do you realise how many people have tried?" I enquired and he shook his head, "Some people have

tried before and no-one has managed it, why are we going to be any different?"

"Oh, come on Alina, where's your sense of positivity and exploration?" Damon laughed and placed his arm over my shoulder, "I've always loved looking at the history of where I've been with my dad, you know, makes it feel a bit more like home."

"No, I completely understand that, makes you feel as if you've been there your entire life," I sympathised and he nodded his head.

"Exactly," he grinned.

"Have you written it down?" I asked and I was handed a scrap of paper.

My eyes scanned over the piece of paper, taking in the familiar words that I had known my whole life. Even I had to admit I was curious about what the words meant but I had known people try all my life and nobody had figured it out. Alexa always jokes someone just carved it in as a laugh and it is just complete nonsense so people would spend their lives looking for something that wasn't real. Still, that sounded more hopeful than the idea of it being a witch's curse.

"Some people believe it's a witch's spell," I tested and he shrugged.

"Either way, I want to find out," he grinned and my heart melted instantly.

Our feet strolled along the paved pathways of the town as the business traffic of the day ceased to exist. A couple of people smiled and waved as they drove past as I did the same. I think it was only just becoming apparent to Damon that everyone knew

One for Sorrow

everyone in Eastmere, it was a quiet town, it was probably one of the reasons why we don't see many new people. The vibrant tops of the trees were visible over the buildings, allowing for the forest to always be insight. A thick fog suffocated the town, creating an eerie atmosphere. We walked in a comfortable silence until we arrived at the town's library. It almost felt like it was night in the town with how deserted the streets were and how dark the fog seemed to make everything. A shiver passed down my spine as the leaves in the town centre rustled around us, almost as if there was somebody with us.
"I'll start in the west wing," he told me and I nodded with a grumble.

When I arrived, I immediately noticed Adrian sitting in the corner with Bridget. The light above them flickered ominously, shrouding them in darkness every now and again. They both huddled over an old black book with an intense look on their faces. Both of their lips moved in a stream of conversation as they nodded sharply at each other's words. I decided to leave them to it, knowing it was best I didn't become involved in whatever the two of them were doing. I couldn't deny the curiosity that had filled me though, wondering what it was they had been up to since the beginning of the school year. Slowly, walking down the aisle my eyes scanned the books searching for anything related to the towns history at all.

Despite my decision to leave them alone, my book scanning duty drew me inevitably closer to Adrian and Bridget. Their whispered conversation appeared to have progressed to a heated discussion. I frowned. The book they were reading and discussing was clearly incredibly old; the leather binding was fraying and the pages were yellowed with age. The book was small and a dark colour I couldn't decipher from my angle.

I felt something move beneath my hand and then heard a book slam on the floor with a stark, loud thud in the contrast to the quiet library. My knees lowered me gently to the ground as I moved to pick the book up, feeling eyes burning a hole through the back of my head as I did so.

***

(Adrian)

A sharp sound made me and Bridget snap our heads up, cutting us off mid-sentence. I took a rare deep breath to scent the air. A familiar scent was on the stale library air; a human one, female, floral with a hint of something else. Alina was here.
"Alina's here," I whispered, keeping my voice low.
"I know," Bridget answered, her purple eyes swirling in their dark depths.

Her eyes drew me in, almost hypnotising me until our noses were just brushing against each other's. "Kiss me," her voice was almost soft it was lost to the air.

When I did not move, she moved forward and connected our lips. If my heart still beat, blood would have flooded to my cheeks. Public intimacy was something I was still unused to. Her lips were soft and plump, tasting of strawberry mints. My demon recoiled in disgust at the taste of another creature but I did not care. She pulled away and I kicked back, something startling me.

"Adrian," the sound of two female voices filled my ears.

"Alina," I heard Bridget greet as the two shared a brief hug.

"Adrian, are you okay?" Alina asked, offering me a hand to help me up.

Usually, I can stand up on my own but something was making me feel weak. Graciously, I took her hand and pulled myself up from the chair. I wondered how much she had seen but she did not seem to be acting any differently.

"Alina- oh Adrian, Bridget," Damon cut himself off as he spotted the three of us huddled in a corner, "Surprised to see you two here."

"Likewise," Bridget replied and my eyebrows furrowed at the language she used.

"What are you two doing?" Alina enquired.

"Oh, my aunt found this book and we were looking through it," she grabbed the book of shadows and safely tucked it into her messenger bag.

"We were trying to translate the script on the statue but the library doesn't have any books on it," Damon explained and I felt Bridget tense beside me.

"You might as well drop it," she voiced, "You're tampering with something that doesn't need to be tampered with."

Tension hung thick in the air as Bridget warned Damon but a smile remained on his lips. I think he underestimated the seriousness behind Bridget's

One for Sorrow

words. Alina seemed to be confused about the current situation so I stepped into the conversation to try and provide peace. Damon and Alina could never know the truth. We were pretty careless about where we sat in theory, near the door to the library we were almost guaranteed to be spotted by someone. Leaves rustled nearby the entrance to the door and we all looked around, almost as if hell was going to descend on us.
"Are you two busy then?" I cut in.
"Yeah, Alina agreed to go on a date with me," Damon grinned as he loosely slung his arm over Alina's shoulder.
"Ooh, do you want to get ready at mine, Mom just bought me the ideal dress," Bridget offered, her mood seemingly changing in the blink of an eye and Alina nodded eagerly, "Do you want to go now?"
"Sure," Alina agreed and Bridget passed me her bag. "I'll call you later," Bridget held a silent message in her eyes and I nodded.

Bridget and Alina left together as they spoke in a casual conversation. Damon smiled to me as we made our way outside to be faced with the town's statue. I slung Bridget's black back over my shoulder, grasping the strap with my hand tightly.
"I think Bridget thinks it's a curse from the way she spoke," Damon started, "Do you believe it?"
"I do not know, some say that Anna McCrea placed the curse before she was killed," I admitted honestly, "I can presume that no-one will ever know though."
"I wonder," he whispered.

Both of us stared at the stone statue, before he bid me goodbye with a wave. I approached the stone

One for Sorrow

statue, my dark eyes landing on the magpie as it towered over me, almost menacingly. His eye twinkled ruby in the sunlight and a wave of fear washed over me. The feeling of another presence arrived beside me. My body froze and something changed in the magpie's eye, something flashing before me and I stumbled back, tripping over my feet. As my eyes stared at the magpies, something was exchanged between the two of us. The bag with The Book of Shadows in it fell beside me.

I lost control of my body; people stared at me as if I was a monster, as if they knew the truth. My fangs forced their way down and pierced my lower lip, the taste of copper filling my mouth. I tried to move out of the town centre and into the forest but my legs became stuck. My eyes closed as a burning sensation caused my throat to heat up as if someone had stuck a red-hot poker down it. I could feel the fires of hell burning into my eyes.

My body forced its way through a door so I could latch onto the first living thing in sight. A shrill scream consumed the air as my fangs bit into the person's jugular. My body lost all feeling until the person beneath me writhed in pain and I let them go, watching the body slump to the floor in the darkness with a deafening thud. Before I could see the damage, I had done, I left. I couldn't look at my victim, the idea of what I just did made me sick to the stomach, I did not need to be consumed with more guilt even though I deserved it. Using the back of my hand, I wiped my mouth and the foreign sensation left my body. I was tampering with something dangerous, the curse was real, it was something very real.

Chapter Thirteen- Alina

"You said something about a dress?" I asked as I walked into Bridget's spring-coloured room.
"Yeah, I'll go get it," she announced, although her voice sounded subdued.

I sat down on her red rose themed duvet and leaned back, as comfortable in Bridget's home as I was in my own. The sun shone brightly through her lime green curtains and created streaks through her lilac rug. Soft fur brushed against my legs as Bridget's black cat purred deep in her chest. I scratched her gently behind her ears as she rubbed her head against my leg affectionately.
"Hey girl," I murmured to her, scooping her and placing her into my arms, "How are you Sooty? Where were you the other night?"

She purred deeper and a smile twitched onto my lips as Sooty nestled into my arms. Bridget arrived back into the room and smiled softly at the two of us.
"You can put it on in the bathroom but I'll have to zip it up for you," she explained, laying the dress on the bed next to me before moving to sink into her desk chair. She seemed subdued, rare dark circles were under her eyes and her shoulders sagged. Her eyes looked tired, it was one of the first times I had seen Bridget in a vulnerable state like she was. Sooty

jumped from my lap and onto Bridget's desk, curling up on to a pillow that had been left for her. She started to stroke Sooty absentmindedly.

"Are you okay?" I asked.

"I'm fine," she replied, lifting her face to meet my eyes and smiled.

"You know you can tell anything, right Bridget?" I moved and enveloped her in a hug. Her slim arms moved around my waist and squeezed me back.

"I'm fine Alina. Really," she added, a small smile pulled at the corners of her mouth and I nodded, "Now go and try the dress on."

I shot her a wide grin before moving into the connecting bathroom, hanging the dress on the back of the door. The dress was gorgeous and it was immediately apparent on why Bridget's Mom had chosen the dress. I managed to get myself into the sleeves and sighed. I folded the clothes I had just shed carefully before leaving the room to meet Bridget.

She was sat on her bed, staring at her fingernails as she filed them. I couldn't help but feel as if she was keeping a secret from me. Something happened to her and Adrian; I could tell by the way they are with each other and how it's changed.

"Oh sorry," she apologised and stood up to greet me.

My hands wrapped around my hair and pushed it past my shoulders. The sound of the zipper easing up reached my ears and I smiled, perfect fit.

"It looks gorgeous on you," she gave a sad smile.

"I bet it looks better on you," I replied, brushing the dress gently and enjoying the feel of the smooth fabric.

"Nah, it was made for you," she smirked, "You always did have the bigger bust."

I gasped and smacked her arm playfully. Bridget dodged me, as light on her feet as if she had wings. The look of happiness on her face quickly faded as she looked at me, her eyes trained on my face. It was almost as if she was remembering something, something troubling. I opened my mouth to speak but she suddenly clapped her hands together in excitement. "I have the perfect idea for your hair!" she announced as she suddenly danced to the other side of the room, "Sit!" she ordered me and pointed to her stool.

I sat obediently, apprehensive about the possible implications this could mean for me. My eyes met her reflection in the mirror as she stared down at my hair, almost as if she was waiting for it to burst into flames or something.

"Right, I'm going to start with a French braid," she muttered to herself as she pulled my hair, her carefully fingers weaving their way, twisting and pulling.

Twenty minutes later, Bridget reached over and hair sprayed me, telling me to close my eyes after she started spraying.

"Sorry," she sung, I huffed in fake annoyance, brushing a stray wisp of hair out of my eye, "Ta-dah!"

I opened my eyes and gasped in shock. I used my hand to raise my chin and moved my head from left to right, admiring the softness of the hair style and how it seemed to perfectly framed my face.

"Oh my god Bridget, you are amazing!"

Bridget grinned and hugged me, giggling as she did, "Come on, I need to do your makeup."

One for Sorrow

I nodded my head and swirled on my stool to face her. She used the silver handle to pull open the top draw of her vanity. She rummaged around in it for a while before pulling out a clear bottle. Her hand pumped a generous amount onto her finger tips before she dabbed it around my face, rubbing it in. Neither of us said anything as she did my make-up, I just watched her carefully. Her eyes were a dark blue, reminding me of the deepest ocean trench. It seemed that Bridget was drowning in that ocean, she was almost unreachable.
"Let's get you to the Mag's Pie Place," she announced as she capped the bright red lipstick she had used.
My eyes glanced in the mirror and I nodded in approval, wrapping Bridget in my embrace, "I love it!"

She just grinned at me before passing me a pair of black heels. I slid my feet into them before walking through Bridget's bedroom door that she was holding open for me. We climbed into her Mom's car and chattered excitedly until Julie pulled up. I thanked her brightly and she just smiled at me through the rear view mirror. Damon was stood against his Dad's car just outside Mag's Pie Place, watching Bridget's car in anticipation. I checked my make-up in the wing mirror and blew a kiss to Bridget before stepping out.
I leaned against the car as I spoke to her through the open window, "I know we did our meet up on Sunday but do you fancy doing it again this week?"
"Want to talk about the date?" Bridget smirked.
"Maybe," I felt the blush creep onto my cheeks.

She just nodded her head with a laugh and I turned my back to her. My eyes immediately scanned Damon. He was dressed in a pale red dress shirt with

black jeans. He had dug out his blazer and kept the formal appearance with some dress shoes. I couldn't help but let a smile grace my face. I wasn't a usual dater but this was by far the most effort a guy had ever made for me.
"Have fun!" Bridget called as she drove away.
Damon met me halfway and took my hand, a grin on his lips.
"Hi," I greeted.
"Hello," he replied, kissing the back of my hand, and causing me to giggle, "We seem to be matching."
My eyes glanced down at the crimson red dress Bridget leant me and nodded with a grin. I'm not sure I could find any words to speak, a lump had formed in my throat, preventing me from speaking. He entwined our fingers and opened the door for me, a gracious smile playing on my lips. Even if I tried, I don't think I could wipe the smile from my lips, not that I wanted to. Damon held the door open and gestured for me to enter.
"Thank you," I thanked him with my words and eyes.
"Hi Alina, Damon, I believe you made a reservation," Mrs Maguire removed her southern accent to pretend to be posh, causing us both to laugh, "I know it's not much but I tried to make it a bit more romantic."
Without another word, she led us to our table and the smile on my face grew larger. The waitress seated us in a secluded booth meant for two, a knowing look in her eyes. Damon thanked her and gestured for me to sit down before him with his hand. His hand gently touched my hip as I attempted sitting down elegantly, but his touch made me shiver, so I sort of

stumbled into my seat. My face flushed red and I budged up to make space for him.

"You okay?" he asked, unaware of what his touch had done to me.

"I'm fine," I smiled, brushing down my dress.

"You're going to have to give me advice on what to order because it all looks amazing," Damon said as he flipped through the menu.

"Well," I started but paused as I realised it probably wasn't the best idea to order my usual, a half-pound burger, fries, and extra cheese.

I need to make an impression and it shouldn't be that kind. I thought about pasta or lasagne, but they have onions and if he tries to kiss me then that will end badly. My choices were reduced to salad, I didn't want to be one of them girls but I didn't want to scare Damon off. His eyes met mine over the white menu and they were filled with their usual glint. The look on his face just reminded me of how interested he was in me and any worries about what I should have ordered just disappeared.

"Your usual half pound burger?" the waitress asked me as she approached the table, my cheeks reddened slightly but I held my own.

Damon said nothing for a couple of seconds as the waitress strode towards our table. She tucked a stray bit of hair behind her ear before grabbing her notepad and pen from her apron pocket and looking at me expectantly.

"Do you have a quorn burger at all?" Damon questioned and when the waitress nodded her head he folded his menu up in a sense of finality, "Two of them then please, one with quorn though."

I looked up to him and he looked down, my mind was drawn to his mouth like a flame attracting a moth. Before our lips could connect, the sound of glasses being placed on the table reached my ears, I don't think I'll ever manage to kiss him.
"Two strawberry milkshakes on the house," the waitress smiled and we both thanked her kindly.

I took a sip and my mouth exploded in a milky, creamy strawberry supernova. I sighed and licked away the froth from my upper lip. I moved my gaze to Damon who seems to have just had a similar experience because his pupils had dilated in a sugary shock and a wild look has taken over his eyes. Pink residue had made a home for itself on his face too and before he could do anything about it, I leant forward and kissed him.

He tensed at first and I began to lean back when he crushed his mouth to mine. I relaxed and leaned into him, inhaling his wonderful clean-man smell and allowing it to intoxicate my senses. The sweet creamy sensation of the strawberry milkshake intensified the moment and I released a dreamy sigh.

Damon's head moved to cup the back of my head, his surprisingly delicate fingers weaving their way through my hair, pulling and teasing gently. His other hand moved behind me to land gently on the small of my back, sending thrills of exhilaration down my spine.

One for Sorrow

Everything else around me fizzled out into white noise; the only thing grounding me was his mouth on mine.

I felt like wings of emotion had burst from me and lifted me high into the sky to a place I had never been to before. I had kissed a boy before, but it had never felt anything like this. This was something else. This was real.

Gently, we pulled ourselves away but stayed close to each other, almost afraid of straying too far from each other. It took a while to compose myself before I managed to open my eyes. I found Damon's brown orbs fixed on my own and my breathing hitched.

Before we could say anything, two plates were placed in front of us.
"Thank you," I mumbled quietly, my voice not quite with me yet.

We ate our meals peacefully, sharing the odd word in conversation and I found the half-pound burger seeming larger than usual. I was starting to struggle when the burger was gone but I was facing a huge mountain of fries. Damon left a couple of fries but I left a quarter of the fries which was highly unlike me. The presence of butterflies had invaded my stomach and I knew if any more food passed my lips I would regret it later in the evening. Damon had a big effect on me, that was clear to see considering I couldn't finish my food. He smiled at me brightly and I grinned back at him from where he sat next to me. The moonlight hit Damon's tanned skin beautifully and he seemingly glowed.

One for Sorrow

"Can I ask you a question?" I asked wearily.
"Of course," Damon replied.
"You don't talk a lot about your Mom, is there any reason in particular?" I didn't want to be too blunt with it but the curiosity had been eating away at me slowly.
"Yeah, she was a drug addict," Damon nodded his head solemnly, "I can remember my Dad crying most nights and the arguments were horrendous. Then one day, she just never came home, died of an overdose. Dad became quite distant after it all happened, that's why I don't like to spend much time in the house, it gets lonely. Atlas keeps me company though, I feel dogs are a man's best companion."
"I'm so sorry," I placed an arm tenderly on his shoulder.
Before I could get any more words out the waitress approached us, "Any desserts."
"Just the check please," Damon smiled and he followed the waitress to the bar to pay before I could get a word in about paying for my half. I think he could tell by the pile of chips on my plate that I didn't want anything else to eat.

    I managed to get out of the booth graciously as I met Damon at the door. I looked at him for a moment, almost as if he was going to burst into tears at the words regarding his Mom but he seemed his usually cheery self. He grinned brightly at me and we slowly began to walk away from the diner and away from our first date. Silence hung thick in the air but it wasn't awkward, it was peaceful. Crickets chirped softly into the evening air as insects buzzed around the flowers that decorated the area around the diner. The

atmosphere was calming and I felt content in the date and myself. The night didn't bother me how in the slightest, I felt safe in the glow of the diner.
"Did I ruin the date by kissing you?" Damon asked softly, "Or should I say by kissing you back?"

Blood rushed to my cheeks simply by the memory and I looked down.
"No, it's just-" I paused when I struggled to find the words to say, "Can I be honest?" I waited for him to answer and he nodded gently, "I've never been interested in dating before but sort of felt like I had to entertain the idea because of the head cheerleader title. It's something the student body expects but nobody ever really interested me. I always figured that something at my age wouldn't be forever and I don't know. I guess you could say I've kissed quite a few boys but never have I ever felt like this before."

Damon paused before saying anything, almost killing me instantly. He tasted his words before he spoke them, being careful not to say the wrong thing.
"Is that a good thing?" He enquired.
Without hesitation, I answered, "It's a very good thing, I'm just in unknown territory."

Damon breathed out a sigh of relief which he tried to cover with a light chuckle at my words, leaving it to me to initiate the kiss. I replied to his silent question fully and captured his lips in mine. We stood for what felt like a century, exchanging passion that together we kindled into a blazing hot inferno. My phone buzzed in my pocket. I broke the kiss with an airy giggle as I reached down to silence it. Damon

pressed his lips again to mine for a while until he finally pulled back.
"I should probably take you home," he whispered, glancing nervously at his watch.
"Probably," I muttered in disappointment.
"Your Dad did warn me about your curfew," Damon mumbled to himself but I still heard.
"Really?" I laughed and when he nodded sheepishly, I laughed harder.

Damon reached for my hand, interlacing his fingers with my own and a content sigh left my lips. We talked about anything and everything on the way home, seemingly filling each other on the events that led us up to the people we were today. It was calming, walking in the glow of the streetlights despite the eery cast of the moon. Once we reached the end of my driveway, he turned to me with a smile on his face.
"Thank you, Damon, for everything," I said before connecting my soul to his for the final time that night, "Who's picking you up?"

Just as I finished my sentence, Chad's truck rounded the corner and I nodded my head understandingly.
"See you tomorrow Alina," I watched him disappear around the corner after he climbed into the truck and the lights of the vehicle had gone.

I stepped into the house and hung my bag up, shoving my keys in my bag as I did and nearly fell over Sunny in the process. Sunny had bounded away from me and was barking from the kitchen frantically. I paused for a moment as I analysed the situation, a cold draft tickling my arms and causing for my hairs to stand on end. As I stepped into the kitchen shards of broken glass crunched beneath my feet.

    I snapped on the lights and screamed.

Chapter Fourteen- Adrian

I bought the fragile glass to my lips slowly, the sweet metallic smell of my survival filling my over-powering senses. My strong hand tipped the glass back and the crimson liquid sloshed against my already stained lips. I heaved a long, shaky sigh from my mouth as I glanced around at the dank basement I had settled in. The hum of the artificial light that cast a non-natural glow onto my surroundings absorbed my mind. I could not hear or think about anything else other than my lack of recollection of the nights events. Something took over me, something terrifying happened, the whole night was black in my mind, my memories are gone. I raised the wine glass back to my blood-stained lips, allowing for the warm liquid to trickle down my throat.

"Doesn't quite have the same effect Adrian," Bridget giggled, dumping her messenger bag on the floor, "Why did I find my bag with The book of Shadows near the towns statue, unguarded?"

I wanted to feel glad that she had found The Book of Shadows but I was unsure whether I could feel that way with the dark cloud of remembrance looming over my head, or should I say what I could not remember. When she saw the sullen expression laced into all my features, the lazy smile left her plump

One for Sorrow

lips. Without a word, she settled down next to me. Carefully, she wrapped her fingers around mine and brought the glass to her dainty nose. Her face scrunched up in disgust as she smelt the iron of the blood.

"O negative, what happened Adrian?" Bridget's voice was soft and like always, it made me feel safe.

I gulped the rest of the glass down before topping it up again. Bridget knew my drinking habits, what my favourite was and what I drunk to drown my sorrow. Bridget and her family always made sure I had enough to survive without people becoming suspicious.

Bridget took the glass from my grasp and placed it out of my reach. If I wanted to, I could have snatched it from her but Bridget was right, I did not deserve the luxury of survival. She interlaced our fingers and gently stroked the back of my hand. I was expecting a shiver to pass through me or for goose bumps to rise on my arms but it did not happen, I was numbed to all and any feelings.

"I am not sure what happened," I mumbled, glancing to her before fixating my gaze on a crack in the stone foundation of the house.

"It's okay, I'm sure it's not that bad," Bridget whispered to me softly.

I took the glass from the side and tipped it back before she could say anything to me, she did not know what I had done. My hand was too firm as I placed it back on the side, it smashed into thousands of pieces. The fluorescent light caught the glass shards, causing for them to glitter brilliantly in the light as they

scattered across the floor. It was like the stars from the sky had fallen and covered the dank basement floor. Bridget used her other soft hand to cover mine, reverting my attention back to her.
"I attacked someone," my voice was that quiet it was barely even a whisper.

Bridget wrapped an arm around my shoulder and I collapsed against her. My head was swimming in the minimal memories that I had of the evening that passed. I tried to grasp onto them but it was like trying to hold onto happiness in the world, it was hopeless and disappointing. Bridget's delicate fingers brushed against my cheek softly, the soft skin of hers soothing against mine. I leant into her touch, I doubted I deserved her comfort but I could not deny that I wanted her touch to ease my troubles.
"I think Anna had something to do with this," I whispered into the crook of her neck.

I felt her body shiver as my breath brushed against her neck, I longed for my body to react that way, to show a sign of life and feeling. Her eyes reached mine slowly, they swirled in great curiosity, hints of a deep blue mixing with tones of purple. Her eyes flickered to my lips before she withdrew to continue the conversation. For a moment, I wondered how my life would have been different if I had met Bridget instead of Anna. I longed for Bridget how I once had Anna, I loved her more than anything that was living on this empty earth.
"Anna? As in the Anna?" Bridget frowned and continued to stroke my hair before speaking, "How

could she have done that? I did not think she was with us anymore or that she had been in a long time."

"I do not know," I confessed as I propped myself up again, "But I cannot think of any other way. I feel like something in Eastmere has changed, like the night we-"

"Found the cave? I felt it too, the air and atmosphere of the whole town changed, almost as if it had become alive. What did you do with the book and the medallion?"

"I have been reading Anna's texts, and they trouble me. She was so angry and afraid of what she was doing to James and being caught. But at the same time, she loved who she was and that she had the chance of helping her brother. It is scary to read, it is as though Anna is beside you, reading the words herself. I let go of my past a long time ago, now it feels as if it is anchoring me down."

"And that medallion?"

"I do not think it was just a medallion. I remember Anna wore it all the time after she realised what she was, like a symbol that she was different. It is powerful too, it has her families mark on it, the magpie."

"How so?"

"Sometimes, when I hold it, I get visions of the past through her own eyes, or mine."

"Your eyes?"

"But only when I am near her, always her. It is only a snippet, like a picture from the past, they do not mean a lot."

"Did you write down what you saw?" Bridget's eyes were full of astonishment, the purple swirling.

"No, I cannot remember it well, it is different to when I drink blood."
"I know how to solve that," she said as she stood up.
"I don't know whether I want them to be clearer," I mumbled, "My past is exactly that, my past and I do not want it to invade my future," I looked to her for a moment, my eyes boring into hers before I whispered two words, "Our future."

Bridget held her hand out with a demanding look in her expression. A small sigh left my slightly parted lips and I took her delicate hand in my own, more for the reason to hold and be close to her than the need for help of moving from the concrete floor.
"We need to figure this out Adrian, some bad things are going to happen, I can feel it. The atmosphere of Eastmere feels as if it's foreshadowing the future and I do not like what I am feeling."

Another sigh left my lips again as she grasped my other hand in her soft one. Gently, with the lightest of touches, Bridget brushed her lips against mine. She snaked her hands through my hair, holding me prisoner as her scent invaded mine. I felt my whole body calm down and come off the edge it was standing on. Just as I was about to reconnect our lips, the shrill sound of her phone reached my sensitive ears. Bridget apologised with her eyes before picking her phone up with ease. She held the phone to her ear as she conversed with the person on the other end whilst I pondered on how she used her phone without a second thought.
"Adrian," Bridget spoke softly as she hung up.

One for Sorrow

I knew from the tone in her voice that the news she would announce would be bad. One of her hands took mine and my eyes bored into hers. Apologetically, she said, "I think I know who you attacked."

***

(Alina)

My hands ran through my hair for the thousandth time as I paced the length of the waiting room. A shaky breath left my lips as my Mom and Fizzy rushed in. Immediately, they wrapped me in their warm embraces without a single word. The sight of my Mom's red eyes and tear stained face broke me clean in two. My tears fell one after the other and I struggled for my breath. Mom carefully passed me into Damon's arms as a doctor approached us. His warmth instantly filled me and my shuddering stopped but unfortunately my tears still fell. The image of my father burned into my brain and I shuddered. My brain couldn't quite process what was going on. I could barely even hear the doctor over my constant snuffling but it became clear almost immediately.
"He's going to be okay. He lost a lot of blood but is currently sleeping until the blood transfusion is finished. You can see him but he won't be able to respond," the doctor suggested kindly, subtly hinting that now probably wasn't the best time.
"We'll wait until morning, we need to go home. Fizzy, Alina?" Mom held out her hands. I took the left and Fizzy took her right as we left the bustling building,

One for Sorrow

Damon trailing behind. His fingers were interlaced with my hand as he kept up with the pace. His thumb stroked my hand gently and I felt his comfort soothing me despite my unrest.

Just as we exited out of the doors, Adrian, Bridget, and Alexa rushed up the slope towards us. Alexa's eyes were wide with terror as she led the group and Bridget wore a look of fear on her face as she lagged slightly behind with Adrian. Adrian's expression was solemn, the expression he usually wore on his face but it had seemed to have woven its way into every inch of his features.

"What happened, are you okay?" Bridget suffocated me in her embrace and I sighed.

"He's okay, currently sleeping," I mumbled into her shoulder.

"It was hard to see, whatever attacked him wasn't very humane, he was so scuffed up," my mother spoke as she stepped back from her niece's embrace.

Adrian stepped back, alarmed suddenly, and darted out of the area. Bridget took off running after him and I frowned, unsure of what happened.

Alexa smiled meekly, "Adrian struggles with the topic of family."

Ever since I had known Adrian, I had never heard him speak about his family once. I just presumed that it was something he had left in his past and never asked about it. I suddenly felt awful about our friendship. Every time I spoke about my family, or even when he saw us together, he never spoke a word. My feet took off outside of the carpark in search of Adrian. I found him quickly, he was stood on the outskirts of the forest, being comforted by Bridget. Without a word, I flung myself into him and he jumped back, startled. As soon as he had realised it was me, his arms loosely wrapped themselves around me like they always did.

"I'm so sorry," an emotion flashed in his eyes as I pulled away from him but it faded before I could recognise it.

"For what?" Adrian enquired.

"I never even thought about you and your family," I whispered to him.

His eyes flashed alarmingly and Bridget grabbed his arm. Her eyes held a danger in them that only seemed familiar to Adrian and he recoiled slightly. It constantly felt like I was missing something between the two of them. I would have questioned it but I could read the situation and knew it wasn't the right time.

"No, it is fine," Adrian told me softly.

"No, it's not, I should have taken a better note," I genuinely felt bad.

Adrian wrapped his arms tightly around me which was new, he was never one for contact. Bridget wrapped her arms around me tightly too and I was sandwiched between the two. I managed to squeeze out after a short time and Adrian turned to me. The look on his face seemed to soften slightly into his natural state.

"You are a good friend Alina," Adrian told me, "That is all I need."

"Obviously not, if I was a good friend I would've been more considerate," I expressed.

One for Sorrow

"Alina, you can just forget about it," Adrian shook his head, "Honestly, I am fine, everything is fine."
"No Adrian, I'm serious. It's almost like you're an outsider. I should know better than to treat you that way," I began, "I mean, it was exactly like what happened with Anna. They thought she was a witch and burned her at the stake. I am her descendant, surely I should know not to treat someone that way."
"Wait, you're Anna McCrea's descendant?" Bridget interrupted.
A frown pulled at my lips and I nodded my head softly, I thought she knew that.
"Did you know?" she asked Adrian, her eyes changed colour to seemingly form a jet black. It invaded her iris until her eye was completely a dark black, I knew it was a trick of the light, her eyes were navy, borderline violet.

It was clear that Bridget was losing her cool. Adrian gripped her arm tightly, almost as a warning. It was evident that Bridget and Adrian were sharing some private conversation. I only just realised how often the two of them do that. Adrian and Bridget knew something the rest of us didn't.
"I best get going, my Mom will be waiting for me, I'll keep you both updated, I'll see you on Monday at school," I explained, "Love you both."
"Love you too, speak to you tomorrow," Bridget smiled.

As I walked away, I could hear Bridget and Adrian whispering in hisses to each other. I shook my head, knowing there was nothing I could do about the secret they were clearly hiding.

"Is he okay?" Fizzy asked from the front of the car as I climbed in the back of Mom's car.

"Yeah, it's like Alexa said, he just struggles with family," I shrugged.

"Bless him," Mom expressed as she pulled out of the hospital car park, "He's always been a good friend to you two."

Both Fizzy and I grunted in agreement as I stared at the blur of green as we drove past the edge of the forest. I glanced back quickly to see the building disappearing from my sight. A long sigh left my lips after I sent a quick prayer to hope my Dad's condition would remain stable.

"Where did Damon go?" I questioned.

"He said he was going to go home and that he would call in the morning," Mom replied, "He said he hopes you get some sleep. He is a sweet boy bless him."

"Oh, thank you," I smiled.

Internally, I had a big grin plastered on my face. I knew it would only be a matter of time before Damon managed to win my mom around. I was happy that was the case, there was something special about him, I hoped he would be around for a long time.

"You okay Alina?" Fizzy glanced at me in the mirror.

"Yeah, I'm sure everything will be fine," I nodded my head with reassurance.

I could feel the sorrow I felt for my Dad slipping through the cracks of my happiness but I tried to stop myself from crying. Instantly, I knew I was going to be in for a long night, I just wished I had Damon by my side.

Chapter Fifteen- Adrian

I was stood solemnly in the pouring rain outside Bridget's house. The night should have felt cool on the small hairs of my neck, causing them to stand on end. I ran a hand over them, confirming they were still laid flat and that I was still deceased. Bridget seemed to be the only person who could invoke a reaction in me, I remained dead to everyone else other than her.

Looking around, I could sense the night creatures fliting away or hunting. I could remember, when I was still alive, that I was always amused by the formation of my breath in cold weather. Now, it just seemed pointless. My breath is nothing but a lie of my current state. I was not living. I was not dead. I was not anything. Sooty, Bridget's companion sat from her bedroom window, staring at me deeply with bright green eyes. I saw her mouth part as she meowed, her voice absent even to my hearing. A small smile filled my lips, she really was a sweet cat.
"I won't be long Mom, love you!" Bridget called out before closing the door gently.

She seemingly fluttered to me, her purple eyes glowing in the soft moonlight. A small grin formed on her lips as a greeting before we set off towards the centre of the small town. The heel of Bridget's shoe clicked softly against the cobbled pavement of the town. Neither of us said a word to each other, I just looked at Bridget, not just her appearance but who she really was as a person and what her existence meant.

In the light of the full moon, she looked more ethereal than normal. Her white skin looked luminescent and almost transparent. A glow radiated from her as if she were a star high up in the midnight sky, shining light into the surrounding forest; how she shined a light into my life. Her eyes were like purple amethyst stones against the stark white of her skin- a precious jewel. Bridget was something real, something unique, almost as if God had given me a slither of hope in my survival.

She smiled at me warmly and shrugged off her jacket to reveal a thin halter neck top. The luminescent glow brightened for a second as her human skin seemed to fade away, revealing her true form. Her skin was as dark as the night around us, except for a stark white patch on her front that wrapped around her neck, leaving her face the colour of jet.

Behind her as if hidden under a cloth, wings rose and unfolded behind her. They were beautiful feathered wings that were the colour of her scaled skin and blended into the night around us. Bridget flexed them gently and moved her shoulders in rolling movements, as if releasing stiffness.

It was not very often that I had ever seen Bridget in her true form, but when I did, I felt as if I were witnessing a natural spectacle, like a falling star in an empty sky.

"My parents want me home soon, I have an English assessment on Monday," Bridget said as she tied her

jacket about her slim waist. I noticed her shirt was short and did not reach the hem of her jeans, revealing a slither of bare skin. I swallowed out of old habits.
"I know, so do I," I started, but stopped after a pointed look from Bridget reached me.
"You don't need to sleep before the assessment."
"Yes, right you are," I started again, "I wanted to know if your family knew about a potion that could help Alexa."
"Jeez Adrian-"
"I know but after what I did to Alina's father tonight…" I trailed off.
"You feel an obligation to her family because you can't do anything to Alina or Fizzy to help them without them finding out it was you who was responsible,"
Bridget sighed and moved a few steps, flexing and unflexing her wing muscles, "I'll see what I can do Adrian, but no promises. I'm sorry." I knew her words meant more and went deeper than just tonight.
"Thank you, angelus meus tenebris," she smiled at me as she translated the words in her head.
"My dark angel," she repeated, before taking off, and leaving me alone in the dark depths of the forest.

"You see that one? The line of stars?"
"I would if your delicate hands were not blocking my view," I retorted.
"You silly oaf!" Anna laughed sweetly and lowered her hand, "I suppose now you will never know which of these stars make up that infamous belt."

"I will not know if you do not tell me," I chuckled lacing my fingers through hers.
"Then you shall have to live in ignorance until I deem you worthy of that knowledge."

Anna turned to me; a spark of mischief glinted in her eyes, or maybe it was the reflection of the many stars above us.
"Adrian?"
"Yes Anna?"
"What do you think they are?"
"What do I think what are?"
"The stars," she said simply, *"What do you think the stars really are?"*

Anna's question left me thinking for days without giving her an answer. It hung heavy in the space between us as I wondered what type of answer she wanted. Anna had asked me what I thought they were, not what they actually were. She had asked me, no-one else.

It was two weeks after Anna had asked me that I had an answer.
"Angels," I said by a way of greeting when we met again.
"Angels?" she asked in confusion as she wrapped an arm around my waist.
"That's what I think stars are. I think the stars, they are angels, giving us light and guiding us, even when day gives way to night. God is the sun, but even the Lord must rest, so he has his angel's watch over us," I explained.

Anna smiled and nodded as she thought my answer over.

One for Sorrow

"So, if God is the sun, and stars are angels, what is the moon?"

A grin formed on my face, I had already thought of an answer for this, as I knew her well enough to know that she would ask me this.

"The moon is the gateway to heaven, and if you look close enough, you can see-"Anna pressed her lips to mine and kissed me gently. I wrapped my arms around her waist and held her softly without pulling her closer in the fear that she might not want it. She pulled back a few moments later, still in my arms.

"The moon is nothing more than a huge rock in the sky, but I like your idea better."

"If you knew, why did you ask?"

"To give myself a reason to shush you, so I could kiss you."

That happened two weeks before I planned to propose to Anna. My mother had given me her mother's engagement ring that same night when I returned home. She was happy that I had finally found someone and I was too. I woke up the next morning to the birds chirping jubilantly in my ear and a spring in my step. It was impossible to remove the grin on my face as I tied my shoe laces.

Before I knew it, perfection was due to arrive at my door. Patiently I waited, a delicate rose resting between my fingers. The colour of blood deepened as the rays of the sun absorbed into the soft petals.

"Adrian!" My mother called out, "Has my daughter in law arrived?"

One for Sorrow

"No mother, I will just go and see where she is," I kissed her cheek before leaving out of the door, closing it carefully behind me.

My good mood never faltered as I took a peaceful walk around the outskirts of the town. Women curtseyed and men tipped their hats to me as a greeting. A laugh left my lips as one of the neighbour's dogs jumped up at me, resting his two paws on the bottoms of my thigh. I scratched him behind his ears, earning an enthusiastic bark of appreciation. He hopped down, leaving two muddy paw prints on my trousers.

"I am sorry about that Adrian," he apologised, his croaky voice remaining soft, "Get that to Madge and it will come right out."

"No harm done Edward, Duke is fine. He is a lovely dog," I grinned stroking the dog's fur softly.

"Are you okay Adrian? You are awfully chipper today," he commented.

"I am. I am about to make Anna my beautiful bride," I revealed.

His pleasant expression instantly fell into one of pure dread. He rushed Duke onwards and for the first time today, my smile faltered. I shook my head, any doubts I had leaving my head. The silence grew thicker as I made my way to the opposite side of the town. People whispered and pointed, my doubts and fears crawled back. My fears of something happening to Anna were growing alarmingly by the second. I picked up the pace and rushed towards her house. My legs were moving so quickly until I was sprinting.

One for Sorrow

Frantically, I knocked on the door my knuckles aching from the contact of bone on wood.
"Leave me alone!" her tear drowned voice was audible through the varnished wood.
   My heart broke in two at the sound of her in distress.
"Anna, it is me!" I cried to her, "Please open the door!"
   I heard the sound of the door opening before a small body was flung into me. Her soft cries were barely audible as I wrapped my arms tightly around her. I led her into the house away from any prying eyes. I rocked her gently, urging her to calm down as her breathless sobs worried me deeply.
"Anna," I cooed, "Come on then, we can deal with whatever the problem is."
   Her body calmed itself as my words managed to stop her tears. For the first time today, she looked at me and gulped immediately. She did not say anything, just passed me a letter. My eyes read the black ink and my eyes closed. I cursed in a slippery tone and threw the letter across the room.
"It is bad, right?" She whispered softly.
I shook my head and wrapped my arms around her tightly, "No, it is fine Anna. We will find your brother, James will be okay. We will get through this."
"How can I carry on like this?" She enquired.
   I pecked her lips softly and she buried her head into my chest. My hands stroked her hair as I could feel her lips tug into a smile.
"You will be okay," I told her softly.
"Thank you, Adrian," she pecked my lips herself.

"Anna, I have a question to ask you," I pulled away and her face grew concerned again, "It is nothing bad, I swear on the Lord's name. In fact, if you say yes it will be wonderful news."

My grin remained plastered on my face as I pulled the ring from my pocket and knelt on one knee. Anna gasped and her hands flew to her face, her hands cupping it beautifully as wisps of hair fell around her face, softening her features.
"Anna McCrea, will you be my wife?" I asked.
"Yes," she cried and the tears began again, "I will be your wife."
Carefully, I slid the ring onto her finger and she flung her arms around my neck. Tenderly, I kissed her head as the smile on my face grew.
"Wake up Adrian. The sun is coming, wake up!"

I was laid on my back in the leaf litter, with a silver wolf stood over me.
"Alexa," I said, bolting up suddenly.

The wolf grinned at me, flashing teeth, Alexa sat down and nudged my arm then looked upwards towards the sky. I groaned as I twisted where I was resting, following her gaze. The sky had lost its dark edge and was beginning to give way to the dawn. Brilliant shades of red broke across the sky, highlighting each and every cloud almost to look as if they were dripping in blood. It was beautiful to see. However, I could not help but feel as if the town was foreshadowing something.
"Thanks," I said, giving her a smile.

One for Sorrow

Alexa shook her head and stood up, pacing in a circle, and pawing at her head. The wolf's body outline became shaky as she whined deep in her core. Slowly, the whine became a moan as the wolf became a girl. Alexa was on her hands and knees, panting heavily, trying to regain control. I wanted to help her but I knew for a fact that she probably would have just slapped my hand away and refused all help.
"D-do you have any water?" she rasped.
"No, sorry," I replied sincerely.
"Figures," she huffed, moving into a crouch in an attempt to cover herself, "Can I at least have your jacket? It's freezing."

I was not sure if the shake in her voice was from the cold or her body being weak from the shift. I shrugged off my coat and watched shamelessly as she pulled it on, zipping it up to the top.
"Well, I'll see you in school vamp-boy," Alexa announced as she stood up. My coat just brushed her knees. She looked back in the direction of the rising sun, "You'll get your jacket back then."
"Wait, I saw a vision of you and Harrison," I revealed and she turned back towards me, a frown on her face.
"What do you mean?" Alexa questioned, confusion laced into her tone.
"Sometimes when I drink blood, I can see a memory of the person it came from. I clearly had a bag of Harrison's blood. I just wanted to know why you do it?" I asked, the expression in my voice was almost sympathetic, I hoped I could get through to her.
"I'm a wolf, wolves go into heat and they need release. I can't change from craving sex at one point to not

wanting it in a few weeks. I had to keep that impression up, it was all or nothing," She shook her head, "I don't particular like what I am Adrian but my human persona is what keeps me alive. So I let the school, my family, my cousins think I'm a slut because it's a whole lot easier than the truth."

"Why do you want my attention so much?" I continued my questioning.

"I'm not interested in you in that way, that'd be gross. For one you're a leech, just not interested in that. Besides, you're also my great however many times grandad, that's a boundary crossed. I want to know about Anna and the curse, see what you know about it," Alexa was truthful, "I figured you were married to her so you had to know something."

"Why did you not just ask me what I knew?"

"Was that really an option Adrian?"

"Do you believe in the curse Alexa?"

"It's inevitable," she shot back, a look of sorrow crossing all of her features.

    With that, she turned around and broke into a gentle run in the direction of town, leaving me once again, alone in the woods. I pondered over what Alexa had said as I headed back towards the house I had been staying in. She was right, Anna's curse was inescapable and I was at its mercy.

Chapter Sixteen- Alina

"How are things?" Bridget enquired as she swirled the straw around the edge of the glass.

I pushed the fries distastefully away before taking a sip of my milkshake.

"Coping, well trying to," I answered honestly, "It's just been a long two days."

"I guess it kind of ruined your date night," Bridget sympathised.

"Yeah, that much has happened I've barely even managed to process it all," I admitted.

"It's understandable," Bridget grabbed my hand from across the table. I shot her a smile, it was nice to know that she was there for me. I always knew she would be but it's nice for her to reinforce it sometimes.

"The date was lovely too, he was such a gentleman and he was really sweet to me," I grinned with a small blush hitting my cheeks, "Even Friday night and Saturday yesterday, he was really sweet to me, and Mom and Fizzy as well. I can tell my Mom approves and when Dad hears what he's done for us, I'm sure he will too. He made lasagne for us yesterday."

"Vegetarian?" Bridget laughed.

"Of course," I shook my head as I remembered the dinner disaster from a couple of weeks ago.

One for Sorrow

"Your smitten," she laughed as she popped a fry in her mouth.
"It's nice to know, to finally feel like this about a guy. This thing I have with Damon is different to anything I've ever felt, like with the guys I've been with before. No-one has ever made me feel like this. Sort of makes me almost feel normal in a sense, like I always wondered why no other guy really turned my head and I guess now I know," I could feel the words pouring out of my mouth, a catharsis that was needed, after everything that had happened.
"You know you don't need a man to define you right, you're badass as you are," Bridget smiled.
I laughed at her, "Oh I know. I'd be fine without Damon but now I've had him it almost feels like I'd be lost if he was gone, you know?"
"You sound happier, it's almost like you've got a healthy glow to you as well," Bridget commented.
"Really?" The disbelief just dripped from my response but she nodded to reassure me.
    Maybe Damon and I were different, maybe he was my happy ever after, like Dad was to Mom all those years ago.

A small smile twitched onto my face as I watched Mom's and Fizzy's chests rise and fall gently in their peaceful slumber. Carefully, I eased myself from the edge of the bed without disturbing them before padding through to the shower. The jets of water pummelled my skin in a soothing, continuous stream. As the water flowed over my body I felt some of the stress from the weekend melting away into the water and down the drain, leaving me with a sense of relief. I wiped the mirror with my fist as I wrapped a towel around my naked body, shivering as the winter air seemingly creeped into the bathroom. A small smile pulled at the corner of my lips as I observed my appearance in the mirror. I was trying to see the glow that Bridget was talking about but I wasn't convinced. I still looked exactly how I always do.

I opened the wooden door to my own room to put some clothes that weren't pyjamas on. As I wrapped the towel around me tighter, I found Fizzy sat on my bed.
"Are you okay?" I asked, sitting down beside my sister.
"You remember when I was five and you were seven and I brought that baby magpie in?" she sighed, still looking anywhere but at me.
"We made a pact that we would tell each other everything, I remember," I said as I rubbed her back to soothe her.

I could tell she was troubled, her head hung low and the usual joyful glint was gone from her eyes. She turned her head away from my fluffy carpet and out to the window. The leaves of the trees near to the forest blew in the harsh winter breeze. A magpie, chest stark against its jet feathers cawed from a branch. It seemingly glided towards us before swooping up towards the sky and away from sight. Both of our eyes trailed after it and remained on the window for a few moments before turning back towards each other. I could see how subdued Fizzy had become since Dad's attack, I was worried. She hadn't played violin in days

and she usually practises rigorously, I just hoped the anxiety and dread of it all would improve when Dad came home.
"Well, the other night when I was with Reece, I think I felt when Dad was attacked."
"Fizzy-"
"Just hear me out okay?" she paused and waited until I complied so I nodded my head, not uttering a word, "I was sat on a stool and Reece was on the guitar. I was listening to his latest song when a searing pain filled my neck. I went really dizzy and fell from the stool. Reece helped me up, an hour later, I received the call from you."

    I didn't answer her, I analysed what she said carefully. She looked at me with serious eyes. If what she said was true, and she did feel when Dad was attacked then that meant Dad was left on the floor alone for an hour. I shuddered at the thought of it, I didn't want to think of him being that vulnerable for that amount of time.
"There's been other stuff too, I keep having weird dreams or a feeling when things are going to happen. The other day, when I was brushing my hair purple sparks just appeared from my hair and in the mirror there was a woman, girl, I don't know!" Fizzy shook her head and raked her fingers through her hair, "she looked at me and started singing this rhyme. It- it was something like one for sorrow, two for- "
"Fizzy, please. At your age, all kind of different things, changes go on in your mind-"

"Alina, you're not listening to me, don't give me that look!" she sighed and stood up, "I'm going to check on Mom, see you in school."
"Girls, are you okay?" Mom asked as she walked in cautiously, worry creating craters in her skin.
"I'm fine, I'll see you later Ali," Fizzy announced and left.
"Fizzy!" I called out but she was already gone and I sighed exasperatedly.
"What was that about?" Mom questioned, taking Fizzy's spot on my bed
"Just me being an insensitive idiot again!" I shook my head and leant it against my mother's shoulder, the blue towel around my hair falling to the side slightly.
"You're a brilliant sister Alina, especially the last couple of days," Mom soothed me this time, "She's a teenager, you're a teenager it's not always going to be sunshine and daisies. She'll come around."
"Thanks Mom, I'm going to get ready," Mom nodded and kissed my head softly before leaving.

    It didn't take long for me to sort myself out, I wasn't really feeling like making much of an effort. I braided my hair back and pulled on a pair of jeans and an Eastmere high jumper, my usual go to when I didn't know what to wear. My phone buzzed, a text from Bridget saying she was outside after her Mom dropped her off. I locked the house up behind me, noticing Mom had already left to visit Dad at the hospital.
"Hey Alina, did you finish your essay?" Bridget asked by way of greeting.
"Yeah," I nodded.

"Mine took hours, I can't believe I managed eighteen pages about sleepy old Eastmere," she exaggerated, running a hand exasperatedly through her long black hair before we turned onto the main road.
"Oh," I replied.
"Are you okay?"

Bridget stopped as we arrived at some traffic lights and grabbed my arm. The tears building in my eyes must have been more obvious than I had thought because Bridget began rummaging through her bag before pulling out and handing me a tissue. I took it and dabbed my eyes, sighing at the smearing of mascara. We set off walking whilst I sorted myself out, arriving in school soon enough.
"Fizzy's not coping well with Dad being ill and stuff but I don't know how to help her. She said she was coming to school this morning, but I haven't seen her."
"Maybe she took a different route?" Bridget suggested, trying to ease my worries as she pulled the gate open.
"She'd never take the way through the woods on her own and she'd be late if she went through the town," I reasoned, but in my mind, that made it worse, "We always walk to the road, it's the safest quick route so we should have seen her."

Fizzy had a perfect attendance- she wouldn't want to ruin that. An ache invaded my lower abdomen, the pit of snakes in my lower stomach squirming in anxiety.
"I need to find her," I started, turning around to start my walk home.

One for Sorrow

"Try calling your Mom first- she'll be hurting from your Dad's attack," Bridget tried, glancing at the traffic lights nervously.
"Mom went to the hospital to see Dad before I left, she wanted to see him before work and I don't want to worry them- especially dad. Will you come with me?"
"Of course, let me call Adrian first, he can help."
"How can Adrian help?"
"The more the better, right? Alexa could help too? And Damon?"

I nodded my head gently and agreed with her, she was right. The more people there were, the quicker we would find her, I needed to find her. She sighed with relief as she saw the stress dissipate from my body before turning towards me, I could see the cogs turning in her head as she thought of her game plan.
"We need to go hand our essays in first to sir, he'll let us go if we explain," Bridget began, "You know Fizzy's code, right? She told me Friday she was leaving her essay in there."

I nodded my head softly and we headed towards our lockers after entering the building. Tears were filling my eyes again but I willed myself not to cry. My head was fuzzy with everything that had happened. My legs rushed into the school quickly and Bridget kept up with ease. I recalled the combination for Fizzy's locker easily. Bridget retrieved the essay just as Adrian approached us. His eyes looked tired and there was evidently something occupying his mind.
"You okay?" Bridget asked and he moved his head sharply, Bridget gave him a meek smile.

One for Sorrow

Gently, I closed the locker and began to walk towards History. The shrill sound of the bell rung just as we entered the room. Bridget managed to charm sir into allowing the five of us to go. I was surprised he allowed all five of us to go, he usually hated when students missed his lessons. Bridget had a way of getting her own way without making herself appear spoilt, almost as if she could put a spell on people. Damon wrapped his arm around me and led me out of the school, the cold air hitting my tear-stained cheeks, causing for me to shiver.
"What's going on?" Alexa asked, barely audible over the sound of her heels.
"Fizzy's gone missing and she would never risk her attendance. I need as many people as possible looking," I explained, my eyes pleading more than my words.
"Why can't you call your Mom?" Alexa sighed.
"She's with my Dad and I don't want to worry them," I replied, "I thought I would be better off with all of you."
"You're right, you will be better with us all," Alexa agreed and I nodded my head.
"The more the merrier," Bridget smiled nervously.

Adrian, Alexa, and Bridget exchanged a look and a frown tugged my lips. They knew something that I didn't, that much was obvious but I just wasn't sure what it was. It was a weird phenomenon, Bridget and I had never kept secrets from each other, as far as I had known anyway. Bridget and Adrian had always been close, but I was unsure about when Alexa came into the picture, especially recently considering everyone knew Alexa wanted Adrian. Alexa had always wanted what she couldn't have and Adrian was the perfect image of that. As long as what they were hiding didn't concern Fizzy, I didn't care.

***

(Adrian)

"Do you think we should split up?" I suggested, "Alina and Damon can do the area near Alina's house and see if she's wandering around. Us three will check around town?"
"Ring me if you find her, I just need to know that she's okay," Alina's voice trembled and I sighed, knowing how much she cared for her younger sister.
"Of course," Bridget gave her a quick squeeze and headed in the opposite direction.
    I gave an awkward smile and Alexa a flutter of her tanned hand. As we walked away, I made sure we were far enough away before speaking the question that was resting on the tip of my tongue.
"Alexa, can you sense witch on Felicity?" I enquired.
"You can use her nickname you know," Alexa laughed, "Just recently yes."
"It makes no sense," Bridget mumbled, "Anna was around ages ago, why has it only just become prominent in the family line?"
"I can't sense it on Alina though," Alexa frowned, "Maybe it skipped a gene?"
"I doubt it, but I do not understand how you can only just sense it," I explained, "Magic does not work in genes, well as far as I know anyway."

One for Sorrow

"I do not know about witches, but fae are born who they are and have to learn to glamour, I was home schooled until I was twelve," Bridget said, a faint smile evident.

"That still does not explain why you cannot sense Felicity," I stressed my query.

"Alexa has known Alina her whole life," Bridget began, "She wouldn't be able to smell witch because she can't usually smell it. Faeries don't usually sense things like that until their full powers come through. She could be a witch. Alina did tell me that they had a freak accident at hers not long ago when Damon went over for family dinner."

"What happened?" Alexa rose a curious eyebrow.

"Damon was carrying through a pot of custard that had just come from the pan and spilt it on Fizzy when she accidently pushed her chair into him," Bridget explained.

"And?" she urged Bridget to continue.

"It was cold," I interrupted, "It was not hot anymore. I remember Damon talking about it to me in the locker room after gym. He said it was bubbling when Mrs Harrington took it from the pan."

"Weird," Alexa frowned.

"Not for a witch it isn't," Bridget commented, ending the conversation.

      Honestly, Bridget did not truly know but I took her word for it, it did not need to be stressed any further. I haltered suddenly when the scent of witch was evident on the air. Alexa looked to me with a knowing eye and we carefully moved forward.

One for Sorrow

We observed Fizzy from around the corner. She was stood before the town's statue, reading the inscription. My sensitive ears picked up her mumbles and I turned to Bridget. I knew something familiar flicked in my eyes from the look of dread that filled her features. The night in the cave filled my mind, the inscriptions in Anna's cave burned into my sight. This was the final piece I needed to confirm what I wished was not true.
The curse was real, as real as vampires, faeries, and werewolves, completely real.
"Adrian, what is it?" Alexa asked.

It was the first time I had ever seen her concerned for anything or anyone other than herself. Bridget grabbed my hand, warmth radiating across my skin in a series of electric sparks. We both shuddered as Fizzy's voice became more audible. She was transfixed, almost as if she was captivated in a trance.
"Are you okay?" Bridget whispered softly.

Fizzy could still be heard, muttering the words, almost like a mantra, as if it was keeping her alive.
"One for sorrow, two for joy," Alexa mumbled along with Fizzy's quiet words.

Bridget's pallor became deeper and I shuddered deep in my core, she had seen it in the book of shadows too. Oh Anna, what have you done!
"One for sorrow, what does it mean, why can she read the words?!" Alexa whispered angrily, she always had hated the things she could not understand.

Her eyes flashed yellow and I could tell she was becoming deeply angered.

One for Sorrow

"It's the curse Alexa, Anna left it before she was burnt," Bridget told her.
"Well, what's the rest of the curse?" Alexa demanded, "Who's in danger?
"It's the whole town. Adrian could only read the first line. I could get a sense of the remaining lines but it's written in the language of magic, I can't fully understand it, only someone who can wield magic like a witch can see it. I can't say what I saw either, if it's said too often we could mess with the curse itself. It's so strong already and I don't want to make it worse," Bridget spoke in a jumbled mess.

Memories of Anna burned into my brain and I could almost feel a presence wash over me. I could remember pieces of the night it all ended for the two of us and I could feel my heart breaking all over again. This was the most alive I had felt since my resurrection as a demon. I wanted death to take me, I did not want this life anymore. A strangled cry left my throat as my legs buckled underneath me.

"Adrian?" Felicity called out.
Alexa and Bridget attempted to haul me up but my weight would not shift.
"Why aren't you three in school?" Felicity questioned.
"Alina was worried so we came looking for you," Alexa explained.
"I'm fine, just have a lot going on," Felicity mumbled.
"I am going to call Alina to say we found her," Alexa gave a small smile before walking away.

I resisted the urge to cry out in pain as waves of fire invaded my bones. It was a duller pain than that of my agonising transformation that hit me, nothing could be worse than that.

"Go back to school Fizzy, I'm going to take Adrian home," Bridget told her.

Felicity nodded and walked towards the school without another word. She gave a nervous glance back, just to make sure I was okay but her figure was hazy as my weakness impaired my senses. Once she was out of sight, Bridget bent down to my level as I slumped against a wall. She took my cool hand in hers and looked into my dark eyes.

"What's going on?" Bridget's voice was soft, almost like dancing snowflakes.

"I do not know," I gasped as I tried to speak through waves of pain, I was hanging onto the warmth of her skin, "Something is changing in Eastmere, the curse is coming to play."

Bridget's face paled. She knew what was happening, we both did. I was left on the cobbled street of Eastmere, trying to procure a sense of what Anna did all them years ago.

Chapter Seventeen- Adrian

"Adrian, have you seen your sister?" My mother asked.
"Not since this morning," I answered.
I was sat at our small wooden table in one of the solid uncomfortable chairs. I had offered to make a new set over the summer but Mother had been insistent to keep the current set.
"They were my grandmothers from when she first moved to the new world! They are our heritage!" I disagreed but did not bring the subject up again for the fear she would cut off my head with a carving knife, which also happened to belong to her grandmother.
I however had not had to deal with the chairs anymore since I moved in with Anna into her house after we were wed. Since Anna was an orphan, she had the place to herself and it made the most sense for us to start our family there, now with our little girl, Victoria. I had said I was visiting my Mother and she agreed that she would take our little angel into the town whilst she ran her daily errands.
I was eating an apple, when my sister burst into the house, a look of pure terror and fear plastered on her face.
"What is it Sara?" My mother rushed to her and put her hands on her arms and lowered herself to Sara's

One for Sorrow

level. But Sara's eyes were fixed on me, wide and terrified.
"It is Anna, she is in trouble. They are going to burn her at the stake for witchery."

As soon as I heard the words, I was on my feet, grabbing my coat and out of the door. I could not understand how anyone could associate the words Anna and witch with each other, she was the most caring person I had ever had the chance of meeting.
"Show me," I demanded.

My sister grabbed my hand tightly and pulled me into the town centre, weaving in and out of towns people. I could see the pity they all wore on their faces as we passed them. I tried to stay strong but I did not know how to be that way with what was facing Anna and I. Sara led me towards a mob of people from the town, all focused on one person.

Anna stood at the front of the mob, her hands bound behind her back and a rag tied around her mouth. She looked angry more than anything else. A rage that burned brighter than the flames of hell seemed to emanate from her body, so much so that smoke seemed to be rising from behind her. As she struggled and one of the men of the town held her hands tighter against her back, loose strands of hair fell from her braid. I glanced around uneasily, looking for any signs of our sweet Victoria.

The magistrate held up his hand to gain the shouting crowds attention. They quietened almost instantly as his authority loomed over the crowd.
"This wretch has been found guilty for using the dark arts and is to be burned at the-"

One for Sorrow

The magistrate released a cry of pain and clutched his hand to his chest. From what I could see, his hand looked red and blistered, with blood oozing from the worst of the burns. Anna stepped forwards and raised her hands towards the heavens, the abusive man behind her unconscious on the floor, the rope tying her hands together now gone. The wind around me picked up and dark clouds rolled in to block out the sun. The lanterns hanging from the rafters above the porches flickered violently in the wind, yet the flames grew brighter and more intense, growing a deep unholy red colour that sent fear into my soul. My eyes darted around quickly at the stunned crowd, trying to find a solution or an explanation for what I was seeing.
"Anna!"

My voice rang out over the silenced horrified crowd as I pushed my way through them. They were unmoving statues like stone, hard to force my way through the crowd. I shouted Anna again, and this time she seemed to falter, finally seeing me. With a look of desperation, Anna shot out her hand in the direction of the crowd before darting in a different direction.

Just as Anna darted past the magistrate, an incredible power forced everyone backwards onto the ground. I rolled over and pushed myself up, watching in shock as Anna disappeared between the buildings, her long blonde braid trailing behind her.
"Witch craft!"
"She must be burned back to the hell she came from!"
"She is not one of us!"
"Witch! Devil spawn! Satan himself mocks us!"

One for Sorrow

The townspeople were already getting into a worked-up, angered state, cursing and condemning my sweet, poor Anna. I ignored the protests and calls of the crowd and sprinted after Anna, shouting her name in the dimming light.

I was in the woods edge when a sudden gust of wind pulled me into the air and dropping me in the leaf litter, at Anna's feet.

"You should not have come Adrian."

"You- You are-"

"Witch?" she let out a harsh laugh, one I did not even think could come from someone as sweet as Anna, it contrasted against the girl I fell in love with, "No. I am a sorceress of the natural world. I have a connection to the Great Mother Nature."

"Why are you doing this?" I asked in earnest, forcing myself to my feet so I could look her in the eye.

"Doing what?" Living my life in peace among the people of the town? Creating healing potions and balms?"

"Then why were you arrested? Where's our daughter?"

"A child saw me casting a healing spell on a dying tree to repair a broken branch on my way to the market. The magistrate has her I think, I do not think they will hurt her, the town would be disgraced if that happened. Adrian, listen. I am not evil, or spawn of the devil; I am a healer of nature. Remember that time when we were children, playing in the woods and you fell and knocked yourself out? You broke your wrist, and I healed you before I woke you up. Please Adrian, believe me, I am still the same Anna."

One for Sorrow

I watched her, searching her soul with my eyes by gazing into her own and trying to find a sign that she was lying to me, that she was evil, but I could find none. All I saw was Anna, my sweet, innocent Anna. I stepped forward and hugged her, feeling her warmth seep into my body. Anna's body trembled against mine in relief. She buried her head into my chest and wrapped her two arms around me tightly. A shaky sigh escaped my lips as breath left me heavily. I did not know what I was going to do, how I was going to help Anna get out of this mess. The entire town saw what she could do and I did not think they were likely to forget. They had to forget and we had to get our daughter back, it was looking like that might be ruined if a plan was not thought of quickly.
"Well done Adrian, you have captured her!" The sound of the Magistrate's voice boomed across the green of the forest.

Anna's head was lifted with a demonic fury in her eyes brighter than the fires of hell. Her anger seeped through in her every feature and I stepped back, alarmed. She did not say anything for a couple of minutes, her eyes just burned a hole into my soul.
"You are with them?" She snarled at me, her eyes darkening dangerously.
"No, of course not, I-" but before I could finish my sentence she had knocked me from my feet with a gust of wind that came from no-where. A groan left my lips as I lost consciousness of the reality that surrounded me.

One for Sorrow

I woke up, startled. My eyes quickly darted around but there was no sign of Anna or anyone else; it was evidently just another memory. Seeing Anna again shocked me to the core. It had been so long since I thought of her but being back in Eastmere brought back the memories of her. I wondered how I ever managed to forget her, to move on from the life we had together. My heart ached, her eyes still burnt bright into my soul.
"Adrian," Bridget's angelic voice called out to me.
  Her calm breathing reached my ears and suddenly, the lights were on. A low groan vibrated my chest as I eased myself from the ground. The hum of the lights was recognisable as the lights flicker as the lights tried to charge themselves.
"Again?" she questioned and when I gave a sharp nod, she answered with a sigh.
  Without a second word, we left the building, locking the door on the way out as well as switching the light out. I had nothing to say, neither did Bridget. We simply walked to school in each other's company. It was a couple of days after Felicity had gone on her escapade and the school week was drawing to a close. Bridget's presence comforted me, it reminded me that there was someone in my life that was good and will always remain to be good.
"Hey guys," Alexa greeted.
"Hi," Bridget gave a polite smile.
"We need to discuss what's going on," Alexa demanded but I shrugged it off. There was nothing to discuss, what was happening was going to happen, if we discussed it or not.

One for Sorrow

"There's not a lot to discuss, we don't know an awful lot," Bridget answered honestly, "We told you most of what we know when we found Fizzy at the town statue."

Alexa gave a frustrated sigh, one I could reciprocate relatively easily. The three of us turned a sharp corner and the school was visible. Small groups of students slowly filed in behind us as part of the school's body formed into the building.

The school was particularly warm today, almost suffocating me. I followed Bridget towards my locker, she always remembered when I needed something. I grabbed my chemistry textbook and followed the two ladies into our homeroom. Alina and Damon were already seated in our corner. I slid into the chair between Bridget and Alina.

"Hi," Alina smiled and I gave her a small, polite smile back.

I was mentally too tired to make small talk, too tired to listen to the same rant again about the same topics. It does not matter which school you go to, we are always told to conform and obey to the school and its rules.

"Adrian," Bridget shook my shoulder gently and I found myself coming back to reality.

"Today class, we are going to see how different factors affect the rate of reaction using limestone, also known as-"

"Calcium carbonate," the class droned in unison.

The bell had rung and during the time I was thinking about Anna and the curse, the chemistry

students had filed in ready for the lesson. I really had been away from reality for a while.
"And hydrochloric acid," the teacher continued. We will do this by changing the concentration, surface area, temperature and by adding a catalyst."

I had done this experiment before; I excused myself from the class.

***

(Alina)

Bridget moved into the seat next to me, filling the gap where Adrian had left quickly.
"Is he okay?" I asked, raising an eyebrow knowingly to push the topic a little.
"He wasn't feeling too good earlier, I think he's going to get some rest or something," Bridget replied.

Her response seemed a little vague, but I dropped it; I didn't want to fall out with her. Damon tapped me lightly on the shoulder so I turned around to face him, a smile instantly falling onto my face at the sight of him.
"I'll get the limestone, you get the acid?"
"Sure," I smiled and stood up.

I walked with Bridget to the back desks where the acid was stored. She began to gather some of the apparatus we would need and I walked towards the grey tray of acid. A guy in our class in front of me stepped to the side and gestured for me to go first. I smiled to him in thanks and grabbed a bottle, heading back to our table. I was about to slide into my seat when Alexa appeared beside me out of nowhere. The

One for Sorrow

acid bottle flew from my hand as I startled and watched in pure horror as the acid landed on Alexa's bare legs. She yelped and leapt backwards as the acid began to make her skin go dark red, then blister in horrible wounds. I scrambled past shocked classmates to get some water and baking soda. I filled on empty beaker on the side and barked at others near me to do the same. When I realised no-one was getting water, I opened my mouth and yelled at the closest concerned-looking humans and was faced with Damon's confused handsome face.

"Alina, what's wrong?" he asked, grabbing my shoulders. I shrugged him off angrily.

"We need to get some baking soda mixed with water to neutralise the acid!" I said through my clenched jaw.

"What acid?"

"The acid I split on Alexa! Her legs!" A tremor crept into my voice as I pushed past Damon to get to my cousin.

I got to Alexa and threw the beaker on her legs rapidly, she suddenly shrieked and shot back. Her head shooting around from side to side until her eyes landed on me, they narrowed sharply and I gulped. I couldn't understand why she was being so clam right now.

"Hey! What do you think you're doing?" Alexa asked angrily.

"What do you mean? The acid-"

"Yeah, you spilt it on the floor, I was just getting some guys to get some paper towels to cover it up so people didn't tread on it," she scowled, grabbing some as she spoke to dry her perfectly normal bare legs.

One for Sorrow

I knelt to get a closer look. Her legs were normal- wet, but normal. I noticed a bit of her shirt at the trim that looked moth eaten.

"But your shirt, look!" I insisted, tugging it to show her.

"This is just an old shirt, the cat probably clawed it or something," she shrugged, still drying her legs.

"You don't have a cat," I pointed out, giving her a questioning look.

"I mean Alice's," she retorted, rolling her eyes. Alice was her goth wannabe friend in the cheerleading squad.

"Are you sure you're okay?" I asked again.

"I'll be better when you stop checking out my legs, you're my cousin and you have a boyfriend," she laughed as a few of the students came into earshot, probably to see if there was going to be an argument worth watching. The students laughed as well and I felt blood creep up my neck and onto my cheeks at her comment.

"Come on Alina. We need to wipe that up," Damon said, coming up behind me and grabbing some paper towels to clear up.

"Yeah, okay," I answered walking back to my desk with him.

"Are you okay?" he asked, placing his hand into mine. Warmth seeped into me from his soft hand, calming my nerves.

"I guess, I just-"I sighed then carried on," I could have sworn I saw acid on her. The red…" I trailed off and shook my head.

"Alexa's fine, come on. We'll go get ice cream at lunch okay? My treat."

Chapter Eighteen- Alina

"Hey," My sister's knuckles rattled the door, "I heard about your mishap earlier."

A long sigh escaped my lips as my eyes rolled. I swear my eyes saw Alexa's skin blistering, it was such a vivid red, I was sure I saw it but she was fine. I couldn't have imagined that, I had never seen anything like it in my life. A shiver passed down my spine as I thought about what I could remember. I wondered quickly whether the whole school had heard about the mishap but I brushed it off, knowing it didn't really matter to me.

"I didn't understand it," I told her and she sat next to me on my bed.

"Now do you understand what I was talking about earlier in the week?" she questioned, her eyes twinkling in their usual way.

I could recall the conversation we had quite easily, it was still fresh in my mind from the beginning of the week, especially because of the stress of that day when Fizzy went missing. Fizzy was talking nonsense to me, I didn't understand what she was saying but now I could admit that things were weird. I was starting to see the strangeness of Eastmere more than I ever had before.

"I guess, do you remember at the beginning of the year when I asked you if there was something going on with Adrian and Bridget?" I questioned and when she nodded, I continued, "Well I think they share a secret and Alexa's in on it. I know it sounds stupid because Alexa's, well Alexa but- "
"Shush!" my sister cut me off, "I believe you. We need to find the underlying cause of this."
I grinned, "We'll be like Sherlock Holmes. I can be Watson."
She laughed at me and slung an arm over my shoulder, "You know, I'm glad that we don't have any secrets between us."
"Yeah," I smiled, "Are you coming to see Dad with Mom and me?"
"Yes," Felicity nodded, "But I'll meet you there, Reece is taking me out for dinner so he said he'll drop me off at the hospital."

Fizzy's eyes lost their glint which immediately told me that she was lying. I didn't say anything for a while as I stared at her to see if she had a different explanation. I gave Fizzy a look but I dropped the issue, I knew she would tell me when she was ready. She gave me a quick squeeze before leaving me to it. My eyes glanced out of the window, seeing a magpie settled on the bare branch. It's beady eye seemingly passed straight through me. As goose bumps filled my arms and my hairs stood on end, I shivered. My feet padded against the soft carpet of my bedroom floor as I closed the blinds. The night was pitch black, only a few stars puncturing the darkness.

One for Sorrow

I crawled into bed, and checked my phone. There was a text from Damon. It simply read, *sleep well princess x*. A small smile tugged at the corners of my lips, worries about my friendship group evading from my thoughts as Damon's handsome face filled my mind. I had told him I was going to visit my Dad,s so I wouldn't be able to talk for the rest of the night. Damon being sweet had asked if I needed any support but I said I'd be with family so he just said goodnight. I closed my history book and placed it on my bedside table, finishing studying for the night. I laid in bed, waiting for my Mom to announce we were leaving as thoughts of how lucky I was to have Damon crossed my mind.

***

(Adrian)

"Do you know what Felicity may want to speak about?" I asked Bridget as my eyes wondered over to her small, shadowed figure.
"I'm not sure but she invited her cousin too, Alexa that is," Bridget answered.
"But no Alina?" I enquired.

Bridget shook her head and my eyebrows knitted together as I pondered on what she could possibly want with the three of us. The towns statue came into my eyesight, the magpie's eyes just catching my eyes from the moonlight. A shudder passed through my body as I remembered what happened last time I looked into its eyes. Things in Eastmere were definitely different than when I had arrived.

One for Sorrow

"You okay?" Bridget asked softly, her voice barely audible.

I simply gave her a sharp nod and became still. Neither I nor Bridget said anything as we waited in the soft glow of the moonlight. Alexa's bright yellow eyes shone from the shadows of the trees. She shifted a groan audible from where I sat and strode towards the statue, the click of her heel breaking the silence. I couldn't understand why she shifted like she did if it hurt her to do so. She tucked her shirt into her skirt quickly that she had just slipped on in the shadows of the trees, making sure she had made herself decent.
"Do you know what she wants?" Alexa said abruptly, bringing me out of my thoughts of her second nature.
"No idea," Bridget answered with a shake of her head.

Alexa released a sigh and settled next to me. We all watched the street which Felicity would walk down to arrive for the meeting she had called. The streets were quiet tonight, any day activity being replaced for night time activity, the little that there was in Eastmere. The creatures of the night could be heard in the surrounding forest and it gave an almost peaceful atmosphere to Eastmere.
"Hi guys," she made me jump and I felt my fangs begin to penetrate my lower lip.

Bridget placed an arm gently on my arm, instantly calming me down and we turned to Felicity who held an apologetic smile in her features.
"Sorry," she mumbled.
"What was so important that you took me away from my run?" Alexa crossed her arms over her chest.

One for Sorrow

Felicity frowned as she looked down at Alexa's choice of shoes but ignored it and continued with the reason after taking a deep breath.
"Ever since we came back to school this year. Alina and I have noticed," I froze on the spot, I knew that this could not be good, "that you three have a secret that you're not telling me, Alina or Damon. Now what is going on?"

Alexa burst out laughing spontaneously at Felicity's attempt to be commanding. If this was a laughing matter, I would have laughed but what Felicity had figured out was deadly serious. Though Felicity was not able to be domineering, it was not part of her personality.
"Alexa," Bridget warned.

Alexa smirked at Bridget and rolled her eyes. Bridget glanced at me with a questioning look. I could tell that she was asking me what we should tell her and I also could tell that she understood what I was saying. My mother had always told me that being honest was the only way to succeed in life and Bridget saw that in my eyes. She did not dispute my answer but I knew that Alexa would not be happy. I am sure that she had still not come to terms with her second nature and I do not think she has much confidence in it, despite the façade that she had made. Telling someone else would shake what confidence she had even more
"Let's go to Mag's Pie Place," Bridget suggested, "you're going to want to sit down. I don't know how much time you have either but it could be a while."

Felicity gave Bridget a sceptical look and I moved from the statue. I took a last long glance at the statue before moving on. Alexa shot a look to me, so I would know she was worried, her eyes boring the expression clearly. Neither Alexa nor I knew what or how much Bridget was going to tell her. Bridget's face was neutral, I do not think she knew what she was going to say.

The night was quiet in the small town of Eastmere. It reminded me of the last time I was here. Much of the world has been corrupted by Man's inventions after the Victorian period but Eastmere remains to be one of the few places on earth that hasn't been changed extensively. The dim light from the Mag's Pie Place softly illuminated the pathway before it. The rush of school children had evacuated the premises as the day ended. We found our booth in the den and settled quickly. We had been here so often that Mrs Maguire delivered our drinks to us without asking. Alexa held a note towards her and instructed her to keep the change. I sat with nothing before me as usual, my hands rested neatly in my lap. I did not want to be the one to break the news. Bridget gave me a pleading look, clueless to where to start.
"Basically, we're not human," Alexa sighed rolling her eyes at us all.

Felicity looked at the solemn look which was fixed into mine and Bridget's features and the casual look on Alexa's, suggesting that she was not kidding and Felicity looked to the side in a way I did not understand.
"What do you mean?"
"What Alexa means is," Bridget shot Alexa a look, but she did not notice, "We're not human, Adrian?"

Everyone's attention turned to me. I headed a long sigh.

"I am a vampire. I have been for around three hundred years. I was born in Eastmere not long after it was founded in 1620."

I looked up from my clenched hands to see Felicity's reaction. Her face formed a soft frown; her brows drew closer together like drawn curtains.

"If this is some sort of joke-"

"It's not, believe me," Alexa cut in, demanding attention back to her, "I'm a werewolf. I got bitten a while ago. That's why I stopped coming over; Sunny knew I was something else and makes me uncomfortable because your house is her territory," Alexa shrugged. nonchalantly and sipped her drink through the pink bendy straw.

"That was the summer things changed, a couple of years ago. You started dressing differently and you drew away from us. Your parents were clueless to what caused it but you were ill with a bad fever for like a week. Where were you bitten?"

"Yeah it was, it took a while for my body to get used to the change, hence the fever. On my hand. Here; you can still see the scar," Alexa pulled back the sleeve of her leather jacket to reveal four white circular scars on her left hand, "It didn't hurt much though and they healed overnight."

Felicity reached out and brushed her fingers gently over the pale skin, causing the fine hairs on her arms to rise and her demeaner changed. Bridget reached out and pulled Felicity's arm away and clicked her fingers.

One for Sorrow

Alexa's attention snapped to Bridget and a thankful look passed between Alexa and Bridget. Felicity glanced at each of us in turn and finally settled on Bridget.

"So, what are you?" Her eyebrows creased together and Bridget glanced down at her hands which were neatly folded and resting in her lap like mine were before.

"I'm a faerie, and no I'm not small and don't look like Tinkerbell," Bridget spoke quietly, almost as if she was embarrassed.

I knew Bridget however, she wasn't embarrassed, she just did not like to be judged and at the minute, the three of us were under scrutiny.

"Why is it so important now?" Felicity asked.

Alexa and I shared a concerned look as Bridget sighed. We could not avoid telling her, not now she knows as much as she does otherwise it would look like we told her for no reason.

"Meet us tomorrow morning, in room twenty-nine, we'll explain then," Felicity nodded her head at Bridget's offer.

My eyes glanced outside the window of Mag's Pie Place. I knew better than anyone what it was like to learn something life-changing about a loved one. Anna was good at hiding secrets, very good.

Night had fallen again. My mouth felt full of cotton from lack of moisture. My head hurt, as though someone had struck me down. I pulled myself up to my feet slowly. My eyes darted around, trying to locate the time and date. My thoughts were clouded as I tried to recall yesterday's events. A gasp suddenly left my lips. Anna.

I rushed around the room as I picked up different items of clothing, shoving my limbs and torso through them quickly. My legs fumbled as I darted down the stairs. My mother was sat at mine and Anna's table and she glanced at me worriedly, bouncing my darling daughter on her knee. I took quick strides towards her, kissing my mother's cheek softly before scooping my daughter up. She gurgled as she tried to laugh in my arms as I rocked her back and forth.
"Are you okay?" she whispered.

I forced my feet into my shoes as I picked a jacket up. My daughter whimpered as I placed her back into my mother's arms and nodded to her before I exited the room. I was unsure whether I would be able to speak.

Thoughts of Anna drowned my mind and I found my lungs burning as I darted to the towns cells. I gasped as my arms pushed the heavy door open. The chief's eyes found mine and held a look of pity and sorrow. He knew Anna was the love of my life, but he did not know that she was harmless. No words were passed between us, I just pushed the wooden door open.

Anna was slumped against the wall in her cell. Her long braid was falling out and mud covered her face from where she had been dragged through the woods. I could feel my heart breaking for her, she didn't deserve this. I rushed to the cell and grabbed the

bars in my calloused hands. Anna's eyes found mine for a brief second but she remained where she was.
"Anna, you have to believe me," my voice came out as a simple hoarse whisper, "I swear on the Lord our God."

She turned on her spot, her legs falling over the bed, revealing the bottom portion of her pale legs. She simply stared at me blankly, not blinking. No words left her lips and she was beginning to scare me.
"Anna-"
"Adrian, son. That isn't Anna," the chief said, placing a meaty, rough working hand on my shoulder. The man had been farming most of his life, "You should go home."
"She is- She is not evil," I stuttered.

Anna's unblinking gaze was still fixed on me, completely blank. No hint of emotion dusted her face.
"Go home," the chief said again, gently pulling me away.
"No."
"What?"
"Adrian," Anna said.

Both me and the chief froze, still as the dead. A breath escaped the man's lips, tickling the skin on the back of my neck as the chief whispered the word, "Witch."

I turned to look at the chief and saw a glossy film had taken over his eyes.
I was not sure what to say or do, my eyes were just fixed on her. Her eyes were not as bright as they usually were, they were dull. They reminded me of a forest during a draught, the fierce colour had gone. I

wanted to wrap her in my embrace, tell her she was going to be fine but I knew it would not help, she did not trust me anymore.

"Just leave," her voice was shaky but confident in her request.

"You know I cannot do that," my voice was soft but firm.

    Her eyes seemed to soften at my words. I approached the cell and grasped the bars between my hands. Anna made no attempt to move, she just stared at me blankly.

"I am going to our home and bring you some of your items," I said, "I swear I will get you out of here."

    With that, I took off running

Chapter Nineteen- Adrian

"You're late," Alexa's eyes narrowed at me and I shrunk in my place slightly at the harshness in her tone.

Gently, I dropped the bag onto the desk. The contents made a thumping noise and Alexa's face suddenly dropped in dread, forgetting about my tardiness almost instantly. I saw the look of worry in her eyes but made no comment about it, I knew she would ask, the question was already on the tip of her tongue.

"Is that the Book Of Shadows?" her voice was quiet, almost as if she was whispering the curse inscribed on the faded pages.

I nodded grimly and her eyes pierced the book, almost as if the devil would rise from the pages. Bridget remained silent as she sat in the corner of the classroom, wrapped in one of my jackets she had bought for me when I first arrived in Eastmere. That day was still clear in my head, I had made a habit of wearing 'dated' clothes as she put it, not being able to keep up with the modern-day fashions. She bought me what she called a hoodie but they felt too comfortable for it to be appropriate attire. However, I realised that she wore them more than I did nowadays, but only after I had been wearing them. She tugged on the

One for Sorrow

sleeves so they came over her hands as her arms hugged her legs in a tight ball. Her head lay in between the valley of her knees, strands of her dark hair cascading down the side of the chair. I could tell she felt uneasy about the situation from the demeaner she was emitting into the darkly lit classroom. Her eyes flew to the door as it swung open to reveal Felicity with a puzzled look on her face. She held her knuckle out as if she was going to knock on the door but Bridget had opened it before she could manage to. Felicity remained where she had entered into the room for a few moments, carefully analysing the situation.
"How did you?" Felicity looked startled as she glanced around the dark room. The lights remained off with the purpose of avoiding disruption. Alexa's phone providing the only beacon of light.
"Part of my biology," Bridget expressed with a shrug and Felicity moved to take a seat next to her cousin.

    From previous experience I knew that words can quickly unnerve a person, even if you did not mean to so I refrained from saying anything at all. Felicity uneasily took the bag that I had dropped on the desk. Carefully she eased it from the bag, much more cautious than I had been with it, as if it was the most delicate material in the world. The Book Of Shadows. As her eyes lay upon the dusty spell book, they bored into the letters on the cover.

    Felicity went still. The colour drained from her face and her eyes darkened like jet black stone. She looked like a corpse and I froze in my spot from fear. I felt the demon inside me recoil, almost in submission as I watched her carefully.

One for Sorrow

"Fiz-"
"Stop!" Felicity commanded, her black eyes fixing on Bridget tightly.

Felicity moved her pale hand so that her palm was vertical and facing Bridget in a motion to stop as her voice had commanded. Suddenly Bridget cried out and her glamour fell, revealing her black and white scaly skin, her wings appeared and tore massive tears in her shirt. They stretched out elegantly behind her, as they always did but her back arched painfully with the revelation of her wings. Alexa snarled and pounced at Felicity who flung out her other hand, throwing her into the wall before she landed in a heap, I heard a whimper come from Alexa as she collapsed and my eyes checked to see if she was moving. She was still but her two bright yellow eyes watched her cousin cautiously as she panted heavily. My eyes studied Felicity carefully, her hand remained in their position. I refrained from moving. Her eyes were fixed on the book, almost as if it was drawing her in. My predictions had come true, there was something in Felicity's DNA that made her different. But I was unsure if she was a witch like Anna, surely not. Bridget groaned from the corner opposite to Alexa, resting in a crouch and she eyed Felicity up cautiously.
"Felicity," my voice was calm but almost held the demand that hers had with Bridget's name.

Her eyes flew to mine and the darkness diffused from them, returning back to the pale blue sea they usually were. Felicity's eyebrows furrowed and her lips pulled in a frown, trembling slightly as she felt her emotions return to her. Her eyes darted around quickly, as if she was trying to figure out where she was. Alexa warily struggled to move onto her two feet. Bridget leant against a desk and watched Felicity with cautious eyes, taking in heavy breaths as she regained control.

"Fizzy," Bridget's voice held a lot more sympathy in it than mine had. Felicity almost looked as if she was a doe caught in the head-lights of a car.

"Bridget you're-"Felicity's words failed her.

"Oh, right," Bridget closed her eyes as her lips twitched feverishly. When she opened them again, her purple eyes swirled like a kaleidoscope of colour as her human skin reappeared and her wings fell away into mist, her glamour had returned.

"Is that what you really look like?" Felicity asked fearfully.

"I told you I was a faerie."

"You're beautiful."

I could tell that Alexa was mad at her cousins power over her. Felicity had managed to subdue the alpha. Fury laced around Bridget's eyes as I gathered she felt a similar way about the events of what happened. Bridget was slightly uncomfortable as she stood there in her natural form. Alexa's eyes pierced into Bridget's for a moment before they faded. Bridget and I shared a worried glance before our attention turned to Felicity.

"I-I don't understand," she gulped.

As much as she tried to look away, her eyes were fixed to The Book Of Shadows. Tears were visibly pooling in her eyes as confusion clouded her thoughts, making her emotionally weak. Alexa stared

at her cousin, almost with a knowing look in her eyes. In the moment, Felicity looked vulnerable, she was vulnerable, the book of shadows leaving her open to the dangers of the world. I felt sorry for her, almost as if she did not deserve to be dragged into this. She was too innocent to know the truth, and so was her sister.
"Things are changing in Eastmere," Alexa started softly, "A curse Anna McCrea placed on the town is coming to life."
"I- I thought that was just a myth. A story Mr Geoffries started to get the kids interested in the towns history, so they would actually do the essay," Felicity struggled to speak coherent words.
"I witnessed it," my voice was quiet but every person in the room heard it.
"Adrian, you don't have to," Bridget placed her hand on my arm with a touch only a lover could give.
"I am okay," I reassured but turned my attention back to Felicity, "I was not sure if it was true. I did not understand a lot of it until after I was bitten. Anna was powerful, powerful enough to create the curse, scarily so for the age she was. I think the evidence that has been presented before us would show that the curse did in fact exist. I do not remember what happened that night though so we are clueless on any details."
"But how?" Felicity was fearful.

    I did not want to scare her. We needed a witch or a sorceress on our side if we had any chance of fighting against this curse. Felicity evidently has some magic in her blood, The Book of Shadows proved this to us. Nobody spoke for a few moments, the silence in the air hanging thick. Felicity visibly shivered as she

thought about the concept of a curse and what that could entail.
"We do not know," I said.
Her eyes narrowed at us, glancing at us one by one, "So you say there's this curse yet you have no proof."
"We can sense a change, that's our proof," Alexa retorted back with a pleading look in her eyes.

Felicity's attention quickly darted again from one of us to the other. It became evident to her that we were all being serious. Her fingers carefully pulled the front page of the book away. Her face creased into an expression of cluelessness.
"Where's this curse then?" she enquired.
"We can't read parts of it. The language is unfamiliar," Alexa explained.
"You are all ridiculous," Felicity shook her head, "How can you expect me to believe in something you can't prove. Don't get me wrong, there's no doubt that you are what you are. I just can't believe in a curse just because you feel it. If it was true then surely there'd be evidence somewhere"
"But it's true!" Bridget exclaimed.

Felicity's fear regarding the curse and what it might entail had taken over her rational thinking. Sometimes, denial was easier. Logic states that we would not have told her the truth of ourselves if it was not necessary but she could not rationalise that.
"Without proof, I just can't believe it," Felicity scooped up her property and left the room, stopping to glance back to the three of us before speaking, "I don't know what you want me to do about it anyway. I'm just a human."

One for Sorrow

Alexa sighed and rolled her eyes as the door closed to a slam, "That was a lot of work to get nothing from it."
"I thought she might have had a bit more of an understanding," Bridget ran her hands through her hair in frustration, "Despite us not knowing what she is."
"I'm going," Alexa announced, "What a waste of time, we are pretty much doomed anyway."

Neither Bridget nor I could say anything to persuade her differently. She was right; we are all doomed, with or without Felicity's help. Bridget carefully moved the book back into the bag. I stood up and carefully held the cloth to pick the medallion up so Bridget could avoid getting burnt. My eyebrows furrowed together in confusion at the weight.
"Where is the medallion?" I asked, my attention turning to Bridget.
She whipped around alarmed and her eyes fixated on my figure, "What? Is it not there?"
"No," I unfolded the cloth to show the missing medallion.
"Where could it be?" Bridget stressed, looking around as if it had dropped on the floor, despite knowing that we would have heard the clang if it had.
"Alexa wouldn't have touched it, it meant nothing to her. At least it isn't the book. We do not even really know what it does," I soothed her worries, "It will be okay."

Bridget just nodded her head and walked into my stiff arms. Carefully I embraced her, feeling her warmth fill my body. Bridget made me feel human, she was the only thing left for me on this God forsaken earth.

One for Sorrow

***
(Alina)

"It's been a quiet day," I spoke up to Damon as we slowly walked through the tranquil park.

It was a clear, beautiful day, no clouds were in sight and the sun was blazing. There constantly seemed to be a fog suffocating Eastmere so today was a rare day, despite the bitter wind and cool atmosphere. That just emphasised the fact that summer was gone and fall had arrived, winter coming quickly to take any warmth away from Eastmere. Leaves were gradually losing their pigments, changing from vibrant greens to burnt oranges. There weren't very many people in the park, just a few clusters of friends and families. Damon's hand was interlaced with mine as we took a stroll through the park, sipping on strawberry milkshakes from Mag's Pie Place. This had become a weekly habit for us, something we should probably get out of if we didn't want to double our weight. I was happy though, the happiest I had been in a long time. It wasn't just because of Damon, things just felt different, almost healthy.

"It has," Damon agreed, "I don't know where everybody is."

"Everybody was missing before school and Alexa only visited briefly during the lunch break," I continued, "Bridget and Adrian have been gone pretty much all day. Fizzy was there, but she was quiet, I don't know whether she's still worried about Dad."

"He's doing better, though isn't he?" Damon frowned.

One for Sorrow

"Yeah, he is, should be coming out soon, it has been two weeks since the attack," I nodded my head, "He's been in a lot longer than any of us thought he would be but at least he's getting the care he needs."

"Yeah, I know what you mean. Bridget and Adrian were in chemistry," Damon pointed out, moving the topic away from my Father before I started crying. That had become a recent habit as well.

"They kept to themselves in a hushed conversation over the book they keep carrying around," Damon nodded at my observation, "I feel like there's something going on and we're just stuck in the dark. What are they even doing with that book anyway, you can barely see the pages it's that old and if they wanted to keep it a secret then, they're doing a pretty bad job at it."

"Before I met you this morning, I saw Felicity walk into one of the rooms and when I looked in, your cousin was sat in there Bridget and Adrian," Damon revealed.

"That's weird," I frowned, "She hasn't said anything to me."

"I do wonder what's going on, I'm very curious" Damon continued but suddenly paused, "What's that?"

      I narrowed my eyes to see the large silhouette of something clumsily galloping through the edge of the forest. A frown pulled at all my features as I tried to form an idea of what the creature was but it was unidentifiable.

"I don't know," I spoke slowly as I fixated all my attention on it, "Did someone's dog get out?"

One for Sorrow

The leaves rustled loudly and twigs snapped, magpies leaving their nests for refuge from the disturbance. It's front legs were considerably longer than its hinds, causing it to gallop abnormally. It had a long tail which arched over its back. My eyebrows furrowed deeper, it didn't look like any animal I had ever seen, it was so unusual.
"Let's get a closer look," I suggested as it paused behind a tree, obstructing our view due to the size of the trunk.

Damon nodded his head sharply in agreement as I took a few paces forward. I watched the creature as it surveyed the area it had stopped in. As I took steps closer towards the creature, my vision improved slightly. A gasp escaped my suddenly parted lips as it briefly came into better light before shrinking into the trees, never to be seen again.
"I think we should leave!" Damon exclaimed as he finally caught onto my own thoughts.

I nodded in agreement and the two of us took off in the other direction, binning our half-drunken shakes in the process. My stomach churned as nausea filled my body, I grasped it in an attempt to comfort it. Our legs carried us out of the park and to the stone towns statue.
"It was a manticore," Damon whispered. I wasn't sure whether he was able to talk any louder after that sprint.
"It couldn't be, they're part of mythology for a reason," I stated, standing up straight.
"Hey guys!" Bridget greeted with a smile as Adrian walked beside her.

One for Sorrow

Bridget and Adrian were linked at the arm, I surveyed the situation carefully. I always wondered whether the two were secretly dating or not, I wondered why Adrian wasn't holding her hand. They both seemed quite content with each other so it made me question what was truly going on.

"What's going on?" Bridget frowned as she noted our states.

"We thought we saw a manticore, but we evidently didn't," Damon breathed, "They don't exist, probably some really big dog with an injury so it was walking weirdly."

Bridget and Adrian exchanged a knowing look and my eyes narrowed. I don't care how much they both wanted to deny it, there was something going on between the two of them.

"I'm feeling sick now, I think I'm going to head home," I mumbled, "Probably too much sugar and sun."

"Do you want me to walk you home?" Damon offered sweetly.

"No, no don't worry about it," I shook my head.

"Okay, feel better soon," Damon pecked my cheek and I turned in the direction, heading towards my home.

The thought of Bridget keeping something from me made my nausea worse. I just wanted to curl up in bed with Fizzy for the night and forget about everything, Eastmere was changing and I was not okay with it.

Chapter Twenty- Alina

"Good practise girls!" I called out enthusiastically, clapping my hands together, "Get showered ready for fourth period! See you all later!"
"The best choice I ever made was to join the cheer team. I hate running track," Bridget laughed as she pulled the hair tie that was securing her hair from her face. Her long black hair cascaded down her side to how it usually sat.
　　My eyes glanced to the horde of students trudging in from track. I was glad cheerleading practise counted as a gym substitute as well.
I gave a small smile, "You're just lucky I removed yours and Alexa's suspension."
"As you can see we put that behind us," Bridget responded before gulping back a bottle of water.
"Why is that?" My full attention flew to her as she crumpled her water bottle and chucked it in the recycling bin on the edge of the bleachers.
　　Her face changed as her features slowly started to drop. The light smile that once was in her features had left and she just looked worried. I wondered what was racing through her mind, what her answer would be. It wasn't exactly a hard question but she seemed to be struggling with the answer. Her mouth opened and closed, almost like a goldfish. I knew what was about

to come out of her mouth would be a lie. Bridget wasn't like this, we had never lied to each other before.
"I guess we just came to a mutual understanding," Bridget's words were quiet, so much so that they almost got taken with the wind.
"Yeah, I can believe that," I sighed and turned my attention to my gym bag.
"What?" Bridget responded after a couple of seconds of absorbing what I had said, her eyes darkened in colour as she stared at me, her eyes almost piercing through me like a jagged knife.
"I know you're lying to me," I accused.

    She didn't say anything, she just stared at me, the towel she used to wipe her mouth hovering near her lips.
"Did something happen between her and Adrian? I know you two have been spending time together," I admitted, although I was sure she knew that too.
"Me and Adrian are really good friends- we have a similar background," Bridget said.
"Isn't he an… well. His parents aren't around," I hesitated, unwilling to use the word 'orphan'.
"Well, yeah, I guess. I think it's more to do with how we think; how we see things," Bridget explained quickly.
"And how do you see things?" I pushed her a little harder as I cleared up my clipboard and water bottle, "We used to be close, we used to be best friends and we shared everything! What's happened? What's changed? You know you can talk to me, about anything right?"

One for Sorrow

A breeze picked up and played with my ponytail, making it fan out behind my head, Bridget's hair didn't move despite the wind. My mind flickered back to the night Fizzy spoke about the strangeness that was consuming our lives and I thought of this moment as being one of them. I could feel my heart hammering in my chest against my ribcage like a humming bird.
"Alina, this isn't a good time for this conversation. I have to get to fourth period-"
"Bridget, you aren't makings sense," I said, cutting her off. Her mouth opened like a goldfish again and her dark eyes flashed purple for a split second.

The wind whipped my hair again, but left hers untouched. Neither of us said anything for a couple of seconds, we just looked at each other. I couldn't understand why she was looking at me the way she was, as if I was in the wrong. I was trying to find the truth in her expression but it was gone. Almost like the Bridget I used to know was.
"Why aren't you telling me the truth?" I demanded.
"Can we do this later?" I rolled my eyes, exasperated by Bridget's response; it was starting to become tedious now.
"I'm getting tired of you all sneaking around and leaving me and Damon out of the loop. You've even got my sister in on whatever is going on," I accused. I could feel my anger taking over my mind but I tried to suppress it, there was no point in getting worked up, it would only satisfy her.

Bridget's eyes darkened again and the wind began to pick up. She turned away from me suddenly,

One for Sorrow

the rapid gust of wind seemingly going with her head movement.
"I'm not going to talk to you when you're being like this. You don't make any sense, never mind me," Bridget responded, crossing her arms over her chest.
"Don't bother talking to me until you're ready to tell me the truth," A look passed between us before I marched away. Leaving Bridget behind me.

I slammed the door behind me and slumped against the wall, resting my head between my shaking hands. Tears filled my eyes as I leant my head back, staring up at the harsh lights. The warm tears rolled down my cheeks as I wondered when Eastmere had changed what I believed to be unchangeable. I wasn't sure if I could call Bridget my friend anymore.

"Hey," Damon greeted, pecking my cheek as he slumped down next to me.

I had managed to shove my feelings to the side so I could function for the rest of the day, or so I had thought. I couldn't shake the feeling that I was somehow in the wrong and that I was being selfish. My thoughts couldn't comprehend how wanting to know the truth was being selfish. However, I think part of me was just sour that Bridget no longer relied on me to talk to like she used to, almost as if Adrian had replaced me.

The BBQ pork wrap tasted sour in my mouth and the fries were cold by the time I came around to them. Damon obliged willingly when I offered them to him. Adrian, Bridget and Fizzy were absent, but Alexa joined us. This wasn't unusual as she often had lunch

with us if she was bored of her circle of minions. However, with just me and Damon on our table, it was a surprise.
"Hey," my cousin greeted, dumping her small designer handbag on the bench next to her.
"Hey," Damon responded after a bitter shove of my wrap. Sometimes I forgot he was vegetarian.
"You okay?" Alexa took a worried glance in my direction.

I rolled my eyes as I quickly realised that Bridget must have spoken to her, or the look on my face was particularly distasteful.
"I don't know anymore," my nails were particularly interesting as I answered her question.

Before she could say anything else, Bridget and Adrian slumped down on the opposite side of the table. An awkward silence was cast over the table. I noticed the ironic seating arrangement, Bridget, Alexa, and Adrian on one side with Damon and me on the other. I had to supress the laugh that threatened to escape my lips; it wasn't an appropriate time to be laughing. Damon shot me a glance, worry taking over his eyes, but I pushed it off. He released a heavy sigh before clearing his throat to address the table.
"What's going on?" he began, "It wasn't like this when I first came here. How can so much change in a couple of months? You were all a tight-knit group and now you've been separated. I was worried about coming into this group, feeling like I wouldn't be good enough because you all knew each other so well, like you had been friends forever, even Adrian who has only been here a year. What happened?"

"Just leave it Damon, there's nothing you can do about it," Bridget spoke softly despite her harsh words.
"Surprisingly, I have to agree with her on this one," I looked up to Damon.
"You're both just being pathetic. Work it out and put your differences aside otherwise you'll regret it," Damon shook his head and grabbed his bag before leaving.

      I took a look at Bridget who just stared down at her tray. She made it clear that she had nothing more to say. I was unclear about what I should do; I just didn't know who Bridget was anymore. I picked up my tray with the untouched wrap on it and left the table. My life had been turned upside down in a matter of hours.

***

(Adrian)

"What was that about?" Alexa enquired her question shot at Bridget.
"Alina caused an argument because I keep too many secrets," she explained regretfully.
"Why don't you tell her you're a faerie"? Alexa asked.
"I don't want her to get into this," Bridget shook her head with her words.
"Have you ever thought that if Fizzy is possibly a witch, so is Alina?" Alexa suggested suddenly.

      A silence hung thick in the air as Bridget contemplated Alexa's words.
Bridget shook her head, "I would have noticed if she was."

One for Sorrow

"It took you awhile to realise Fizzy was," Alexa continued.
"Do you think our secrets are safe, what if Fizzy tells Alina," Bridget questioned.
"She's not like that," Alexa shook her head, "She has honour, no matter how much that might hurt her sister."
"I agree," as much as I hated to admit it, I knew Alexa was right, Felicity would not tell.
"I'm off, going to see if anybody else is more interesting because to be frank, this is quite dull," Alexa rolled her eyes.

Alexa gracefully slid from her seat, clutching her bag, and left the dining hall. Her long hair swung from her ponytail behind her as she moved her hips seductively, leaving the boys eyes trailing behind her. Bridget and I just shared a glance, I could see her trying to suppress the tears in her eyes but I wiped the one that escaped with my thumb. She gave me a sad smile before leaving the table and her lunch on the tray. I watched her walk away until I was left on my own, as I always was.

"Adrian are you okay?" My younger sister asked.
"I am fine," I answered her as I manically rushed around the room.

I picked up the bag I had left at my mother's after dropping some groceries off and left the house, pulling the leather strings tighter. My feet moved me quickly as I rushed to leave the house. The people of the town gave me pitying looks as I walked hurriedly towards our house. I fished the key for our house out of

One for Sorrow

my pocket and unlocked the door with a shaky hand. The house was empty and cold; the ashes in the fire place were dark and as lifeless as dust.

I went straight to our bedroom and selected one of her warmer dresses with mink fur on the inside as well as a bar of pine soap and a hairbrush. My eyes darted as I scanned her books, picking one up she had not told me about, that way, I knew that she had not read it.

Suddenly, I paused. A heavy sigh escaped me as my eyes softened and I lowered myself onto our shared bed. How many times have Anna and I rested on this bed together? What stories had we shared? What words had been thrown into the world, words that meant so much for us but nothing to others. Would they ever be said again? We were supposed to raise our daughter together, to raise a family, we were supposed to have a happily ever after.

I did not care that Anna was a sorceress. She was no harm to me or anyone else. It was not fair that she had been taken away from me. She had done nothing wrong. Anna had never committed any bad crime when she was with me, why would she live all these years silently if she meant harm. I just do not understand it, not any of it. I just wanted Anna back.

Tears flew down my cheeks as I bled the liquid of my soul. Heavy gasps of air filled my chest as I expelled my grief. The evidence was stacked against her, she was going to die. Anger filled me and I quickly found myself kicking over her bedside table. The contents of it spilled onto the floor. My heart pounded against my ribcage as a key caught my attention as it shimmered in the light. I was like a magpie; my eyes were set on the prize. The key was cold in my hands, cool metal contrasting against the heat of my hand. I pondered on what it was for and why it was hidden. I grabbed the bag of her things and slipped the key into my jacket pocket.

I moved towards the door and threw it open, I had a brief attack as I came face to face…with Anna. My mouth crept down a little as I gaped at the image of my wife. I was truly speechless.
"Anna?"
"Adrian."
"How are you?"
"I am not."
"How-?"
"I am a witch Adrian. I have magic powers. I am a vision. Now follow me."
"Anna-"
"Now Adrian!"

The vision of Anna showed no emotion and glided down the hall, not breaking eye contact, and my eyes not moving from the vision of Anna. She was eerily still as she glided.
"I love you," vision Anna said.
"I love you," I answered, and followed vision Anna as though I was speaking to the real Anna.

She stopped suddenly, glancing around before gliding into the wall next to the door of the basement. A frown filled my lips but I pushed the door to the basement open anyway. Before I could take my first steps down the stairs, my eye caught something. A passage way was revealed to me. Anna's vision was

One for Sorrow

nowhere to be seen so I took cautious steps down the flight of stairs. Small candles in brass handles gently flickered to life. My path became clear and I began to make quicker progress down the stairs. As I came into the area the stairs led me to, my mouth opened in shock.

Shelves adorned the wall of one side of the cave. Hundreds of books were stacked upon the shelves, all with different titles, different words, different stories. Potion bottles and jars were arranged on a different oak shelf. There was parchment littered around the area, leaves had fallen from a nearby forest and blown into the cave. I wondered how many entrances there were to the cave, I wondered what Anna wanted me to do in a cave. What was I here for?

A shadow shifted as a low groan vibrated in the chest. I glanced around, unnerved before taking off back up the steps, I could not begin to think about what the noise was or what Anna was keeping down there. The door slammed shut behind me, the key burning into the side of my leg as the metal grew boiling hot. I flung it out of my pocket and watched enthralled as she miraculously as it changed shape into the form of a different key that would open a different lock. It suddenly clicked; maybe Anna did not have to die after all.

"Adrian?" I felt Alexa's hot hand on my arm as I phased back into reality. My eyes reached hers and they softened slightly at the look of worry in her eyes. "Are you okay?" Alexa asked, "You've been sat by yourself this entire time."

One for Sorrow

I blinked a couple of times, almost dazed at her question. I struggled to use my mouth a couple of times before I answered.
"Er, I- I do not know anymore," I grabbed my backpack and left the area. Visions of Anna filled my past, visions of my love.

Chapter Twenty One- Adrian

"Anna's presence is still with us, she is doing something to my head, my consciousness and I do not understand," I stressed, exasperated.
"What do you mean?" Alexa enquired, her attention fully captivated.

Our pace was slow as we walked through the quiet streets. The moon cast an eerie glow onto the cobbled pavements as we walked along. Bridget had remained silent during the conversation, a look of thought etched onto every feature. Magpies cawed into the stark night air, almost as a warning. The hairs on the back of my neck rose as I felt the atmosphere around me change. I bit my tongue to suppress the Demon.
"Adrian, have you ever seen Anna's spirit?"
"You mean like a ghost?" Alexa interrupted.
"Not for many years…"
"When?"
"Not since the night of her passing."
"You haven't seen her since?"
"No."
"You're sure."
"Yes Bridget, I am sure I have not seen Anna's spirit since the night she- "I did not finish the sentence.

"It's okay Adrian, I just wanted to be sure that her spirt had moved on," Bridget shot me a sympathetic look and I gave her a small smile.

Alexa opened her mouth to speak but the call of a magpie interrupted her. All three of us glanced to each other with anxious eyes. I could tell they had all sensed the change. Eastmere was resting on a fragile atmosphere, almost as if it could change with one whisper of the curse. Alexa remained quiet for a few seconds as she tried to think about her question carefully.

"How much do we know about her past?" Alexa enquired.

"A lot, but not everything that happened up to her sentence, she hid a lot away from me, and I was unconscious for the casting of the curse. That is why I was unsure of its existence," I also spoke carefully.

"Did you speak to anyone after?" Alexa continued her questioning.

"Nobody would speak about it, it was a forbidden topic to talk about the witches that were burnt," I explained, "Our child went to an orphanage out of the town and her name was changed."

"Who's was it?" Alexa asked.

"We were married, I told you Victoria was mine," my eyes narrowed at her but she just diverted her gaze, "None of this is my fault, or her fault, she was distraught, she thought I was deceased and her daughter was torn from her."

"Now is not the time to be placing fault on anybody," Bridget interrupted, glancing between Alexa and me.

One for Sorrow

Alexa glanced at me and I shook my head, our opinions of each other did not matter anymore. I noted the apology she held in her eyes, even if she was too proud to say it.
"What do we know so far?" Bridget began, focusing on the topic at hand, "About you know what?"
"Anna cast it before she was gone," I started to explain, "I did not stay in Eastmere long after and no-one would explain what happened to me. Our daughter was taken from me. I do not know when and where she went. No-one would speak to me. I was shunned, so I left. Her cave remained untouched, out of bounds, as the town was too afraid. I guess we activated it when we were in the cave. There are no records of that night so it is unknown."
"But what's changed in Eastmere?" Alexa asked.
"Not too much," Bridget replied, "It's been more to do with Adrian. I think we can all admit the atmosphere change though."
"I've always had dreams or visions if you will," I began, almost whimsically, "But they were always of the person of whom I had drunk from, now they are of myself."
"Yourself?" Alexa frowned.
"Of my life before I was bitten, my life with Anna. I've seen one of our dates, I've seen her cry about her brother, I've seen her capture, I've-"I cut myself off. I did not want to think of it anymore.
"Why would you be seeing that?" Alexa asked.
"I do not know," I responded honestly.
"We also don't know where the medallion has gone," Bridget added.

One for Sorrow

"What does The Book Of Shadows say?" Alexa continued to question us.
"Not a lot, we cannot understand it very well," I heard Bridget express.
"Felicity translated the first two lines, which is what is inscribed into the statues base. She said, 'one for sorrow, two for joy' but then could not translate anymore," I stated and we all looked around warily as if lightning was going to strike us dead.

I spoke the first two lines of the statues inscription, what I believed to be the curse. The atmosphere in Eastmere left us all on edge but after a couple of seconds, we felt safe enough to continue our discussion. Bridget and Alexa both nodded their heads in acknowledgement of my words. A magpie cried out again and we realised that we were safe. Alexa opened her mouth to speak but paused suddenly. Her nose twitched as she tested the air. The longer she sniffed, the more I noticed the expression on her face had changed.
"Wh- What is it?" I heard the worry and anticipation in Bridget's voice.
"There's a fire," Alexa announced.
"But the only house around here is Alina's," Bridget replied.

We all looked to each other for a moment before I took off in a run. Alexa and Bridget followed me, Bridget falling behind and Alexa staying just behind me.
"You grab Alina, I'll get Sunny, Alina's parents are out and Fizzy's a light sleeper so she would have woken herself up, if not, call for Bridget," I just

nodded as Alexa fired orders at us. Bridget came to a running stand still when she saw Felicity taking off towards the forest.
Alexa frowned, "Fizzy!"

Her youngest cousin ignored her and continued to walk into the depths of the forest.
Bridget caught up with us, "What's going on? She wouldn't leave like that."
"Quick," Alexa called out, "Alina must still be in there!"

***

(Alina)

Sunny was barking downstairs. I tried to call out her name but choked on a lungful of smoke. My heart raced in my chest like a fox being hunted by hounds. Sunny's barking turned to terrible shrieks, unlike anything I had heard before. My heart stopped for a moment, I had to find a way out. Glass shattering downstairs caught my attention, the fire was getting increasingly worse; it was going to swallow up the entire house.

Carefully, I pressed the back of my hand to the doorknob and felt that it was cool. I opened it and ducked as a cloud of smoke came billowing towards me. Another painful cough left my lips as I heaved up thick black smoke.
"Fizzy!" I called out, my hoarse voice barely audible over the crackling flames.

One for Sorrow

There was no answer. I carefully retreated into the hallway to see the smoke consuming Fizzy's bedroom. There was no way she could still be alive. "Fizzy!" I yelled again, but I could barely hear my own voice over the roar of the flames.

Sunny's frantic shrieks downstairs continued as something collapsed in one of the other rooms. A breath of heat rolled through the corridor and burned against my skin. I cried out, inhaling another lungful of heated air, and reigniting the inferno inside me. My head began to pound as the oxygen was lost in the house. I stumbled towards the stairs, my eyesight hazy as I glanced to see who was at the bottom.

My eyes found a larger dog carrying Sunny out by the scruff of her neck. She wasn't barking at the strange dog that had abducted her, she was calm, almost as if she knew the animal.

Before I could process what I had seen, another violent cough left my oxygen-starved lungs as I clung onto the balcony. The roaring fire almost deafened me as the flames grew and I was panicked that my way out was blocked.

Cautiously, I eased myself down the wooden stairs until a hazy figure caught my attention. I squinted trying to make out the identity of the person but the smoke made everything blurry and unclear. My mind wondered whether it was death, waiting to take me away after the flames had done their work.

I'm sorry Bridget, I love you Damon, I love you Fizzy.

I lost sight of everything.

One for Sorrow

***
(Adrian)

"I can hear Sunny barking!" Alexa announced, "Why would Fizzy just leave like that without helping Alina and Sunny?"

Bridget shook her head as a gesture of her lack of comprehension.

"I'm going in!" Alexa yelled.

Both Bridget and I watched as she easily shifted and I observed as she effortlessly took off into the burning house. Bridget glanced at me worriedly. I interlaced her fingers with mine as we waited for a couple of seconds to see when Alexa would return. The lack of noise coming from Sunny allowed us to know she was safe. Alexa emerged from the cloud of smoke with Sunny. The dog looked happy to be reunited with a familiar face and Alexa lowered her to the ground before phasing back to her human form, taking in deep breaths of air and staying huddled to the ground to cover her decency. I watched as Bridget took her jacket, chucking it to Alexa so she could cover herself.

"Alina's at the top of the stairs," Alexa spoke with a rough tenor.

I moved to go in but Bridget held onto my hand with a tight grasp.

"You're not invincible, you know?" Bridget expressed her concerns.

"I know," I nodded my head, "I will be careful."

"She's not Anna," Bridget called out after me; her words resonated in my head.

One for Sorrow

She was right, Alina was not Anna but I had to save her, she was my friend. With that, I turned and took Bridget in my arms. I gently connected our lips together and withdrew quickly. She breathed a sigh, her breath causing a cloud of steam to rise into the air. Alexa nodded to me and I returned a small smile.

A breath I did not need to take was drawn in and I stepped into the house. Alina's figure was visible, clinging to the banister, falling by the second as she dropped onto her knees. I could see her fighting her heavy eyelids as they closed, her eyes fluttering as she fought to stay with the world. Thick black smoke was consuming the air; Alina was running out of oxygen, out of life.

"Ad-"she coughed, unable to finish my name.

I had reached her in three easy strides; cradling her body into my arms. Her eyes were closed, fluttering still as if she was trying to stay awake. A feeling washed over me, I could see Anna, I could feel her.

"Adrian!" Bridget cried out. I could hear her but my mind was unavailable to register it.

My legs took slow, agonising steps forward. My arms weakened; Alina was beginning to fall. Bridget's eyes were filled with concern as I stood with Alina. I wanted to move forward but something was keeping me back. Someone was keeping me back.

Alina slipped from my arms but Bridget held her up. Gently she was brought towards the ground; unconscious but alive.

The feeling returned.

I had to go into the fire.

One for Sorrow

I think Bridget called my name, but she could not leave Alina. Alexa was holding onto Sunny's collar, the dog was barking and whining and trying to reach Alina. Felicity had disappeared.

I got to the porch steps of the house. The fire had consumed the house like a starved beast, licking at the internal brick structure as if they were bones of a turkey, still hungry for more. Inside the fire, Anna beckoned me.

"Come to me, Adrian. I can save you. You have had enough pain, enough torment, and enough time; let me save you. I love you."

I stepped into the flames. The heat welcomed me like a warm embrace; I felt Anna's love in the fire, strong and passionate and three hundred years' worth of longing.

I love you, Anna.

I feel the fire burning me, freeing me of the chains I have been carrying for too long.

I love you, Anna.

Sound roars around me, but I do not know if it is me or the fire. The inferno is my saviour.

I love you, Anna.

I am almost gone. But I am free from my bounds. I can see Anna, her light, her essence, her love. Our innocence as children was presented to me and the promise we made together before God. We vowed to be together forever, and now it was time to finally to honour that.

I love you, Anna.
I love you, Bridget
I love-

One for sorrow

***

(Alina)

"Alina?"
Voice. A voice drifted towards me. I felt as though I was floating in a vacuum, suspended in dark space and floating, alone and purposeless.
"Alina?" The voice was like a soft rope of silk waving towards me. In the dark space, I reached out in wonder and tried to grab it.
"Wake up."
The silk wrapped around me like a warm embrace. I felt it urging me from my slumber, feeling my eyes flutter open, I came into reality again. Two pairs of eyes stared down at me, checking I was okay. I felt Sunny's cold nose nuzzling into the crook of my neck. My eyes shot open when I heard Bridget's heavy sobs breaking the atmosphere. The relaxation of my slumber was gone and reality was brutal.
"Wh-What happened?" Alexa assisted me in sitting up as I spoke, my voice hoarse.
A rough cough left my lips as my lungs screamed in protest. The ruins of my house were now dying embers. Firemen pottered in the ashes of my home, the sirens of an ambulance faint in the distance. I felt my heart stop beating and my stomach twist. It was gone, my childhood, my life, my memories, then it hit me.
"Fizzy!" I screamed, tears filling my eyes, "Where is she? Tell me she's okay. I can't-"

One for Sorrow

"Shush," Alexa hushed me, stroking my hair as I lay in her lap, "She's okay, she left!"

I nodded my head scrambling to get up. I could see the pain etched onto Alexa's face and the sympathy as her eyes landed on Bridget's. I approached Bridget who was collapsed on the floor in a heap. Sobs racked her body as her eyes were fixed on the remains of the house.

"Don't," Alexa's voice was almost a whisper as she held an arm out to stop me.

My eyes glanced at Bridget as she continued to bleed the liquid of her soul. I had never seen my best friend cry like that before, I was honestly terrified. Her body shook from the force of her sobs and the viciousness of what she was experiencing, dread filled me immediately.

"Wh-What's going on?" I couldn't find my words; my head was still all over the place.

"Adrian carried you out but he- "Alexa gulped and I knew right then what she meant.

Alexa had to hold me up as I processed her words, tearing them apart and putting them together in a way that was understandable. Adrian was gone, that was something I couldn't fathom.

"Bridget, I'm- "An ear-splitting roar was released and my attention was diverted straight towards the source.

"It's the manticore," Alexa announced.

"Why is it not attacking?" I asked, taking steps back from the edge of the forest.

"It wants us to follow him," Alexa replied.

Bridget stumbled to her feet, wiping her tear soaked cheeks, though they were quickly replaced. The

One for Sorrow

three of us and Sunny followed the beasts track as it guided us through the dense forest. I withdrew myself slightly from the lead Alexa had taken, worried that the beast would turn any second. Venom dripped menacingly from its stinger. A thick mist hung over Eastmere, a heavy mist which seemed to suffocate the air.

It wasn't long until we came to a small clearing.
"Fizzy!" Alexa cried out.

She was ignorant to her cousin's words. An ethereal glow cocooned her as she sat straight up with her legs folded beneath her. Her eyes were closed, almost as if she was still sleeping.
"The medallion," Alexa pointed out.

Our eyes landed on the golden object that rested in her cupped hands. We all looked to each other, confusion laced into our expressions. None of us could make sense of what happened but it didn't matter. Under our expressions of confusion, sorrow wound its way into our every fibre. Sorrow was the only feeling we could acknowledge, our friend, was gone.

In the distance, a magpie soared above the tree tops, crying out as it stood out, stark against the moonlight.
Fizzy's eyes suddenly bolted open, "One for sorrow."

One for Sorrow

Epilogue- Adrian

"Adrian!"
"Anna? Where are we?" I looked around in confusion. I could see nothing around us; all I could see was an endless expanse of white.
"This is the next life Adrian, we can be together forever here," She smiled, as beautiful and as lovely as ever. As wondrous as she was on our wedding day.
  Anna leaned forward and kissed me, her lips soft against my own. Neither of us advanced further, we just rested in each other arms, against each other's lips for a brief second.
"I do not understand," I muttered as I leant my forehead against hers.
"I have been waiting for you," Anna admitted, "I am so sorry; I did not mean to do it, any of it."
  I blinked a couple of times as I found my bearings. I could not understand what was happening, my mind was drowning in thoughts and memories and I could not surface. Anna interlaced her fingers with mine as her eyes tried to read my thoughts.
"Adrian?" Anna's voice was questioning.
"What happened? I do not understand the past, how things ended," I was honest in my words.
"I can show you what happened, after James had turned you," Anna offered, "What do you remember?"

One for Sorrow

"It was agonising," I spoke immediately; "It was a wave of fire running through my blood. It was like I was trapped in a fiery inferno with no way to get out. I did not think it would ever end."

"I am sorry Adrian, I did not want it to end that way, it should have been different," Anna glanced down at our entwined fingers, almost in shame.

"The curse, can you explain it to me?" I asked, "I wish things had ended differently, it should not have happened that way."

"I thought you were dead and I was so angry with the magistrates, the town's people, but mostly at myself. I should have ended James's life when I first found him; it was a couple of weeks before I died. I knew what he was, as my mother had spoken of such beings before, and how the thirst controls them. I thought I could heal him, for I am a healer, and I was so close Adrian, believe me. That night, he spoke to me as if he were still human and seemed so concerned and scared…" A tear slid down her cheek and let go of her jaw to land on the peak of her breast, "When the boy saw me heal the tree branch in the forest. I was looking for the final ingredient for the elixir I was certain would release him from his curse."

"But Anna, you still have not explained."

"I am sorry; it pains me so to remember that night. I thought you and James were dead. It was like a darker version of myself took over."

"And what of Bridget? Alina? Alexa? Felicity? What will come of them?"

"I cannot know for sure…" Anna looked up with pure misery casting a gloom over her whole being.

I still held her in my arms closely; I could not let her go again.
"We get to stay together now, forever this time," she smiled more confidently at me now, determined, "Would you like to see what happened after?" I knew what she meant; after James passed on his poison to me. I nodded.
"Take my hand," Anna whispered, interlacing her fingers through mine, electric shocks danced up my skin, I could feel again.
  She closed her eyes and I my own, as we revisited that awful night, but this time together.

A strike of lightning illuminated the whole sky as dark stormy clouds rolled over the hills of the forests. Anna remained flung over my dead body, her tears following onto my paling skin. My heart broke at the sight of her. I wanted to comfort her, to tell her that everything was going to be okay but that was a lie.
"No!" she screamed her woes as the town's magistrate pried her up from me as she sobbed. I felt Anna's hand squeeze mine in reassurance before she moved to follow her past self from the cave.
"You said you woke up after I was," she paused as she thought of the correct word, "Gone."
  I simply just nodded my head. She turned away from me and followed the mob of people out of the cave, leaving my dead body alone.
  The pain that I could remember coursing through my dead body made me shiver. I did not want to remember that time. My eyes lingered on Anna as

she followed the light of the torches through the tunnels. Her delicate hand rested in my own keeping a physical connection between us. The sunlight blinded us as the last rays of God were taken away. Misery flooded the atmosphere as darkness loomed over the town. Anna glanced back at me briefly as my pace slowed down.
That was when I saw it.

Placed where the town's statue will be, Anna's execution place had already been set up. A tall, dark post towered over the forming crowd, hay nestled around the bottom of it. They had not even waited for Anna's trial before setting up; she was always going to die. An infant's cry was audible as she was taken from my mother. Mine and Anna's daughter's cries echoed in our minds as the authorities took her away. It felt like our family had been ripped apart. Anna began to cry as she watched the scene unfold.

I held onto her hand tighter.

Anna was forced up onto the small platform, loose strands of her hair falling over her face.
"What did you do witch?" The magistrate grumbled roughly, poking Anna in the side with a pitch fork.

She whimpered but remained silent, crimson red beginning to soak into her beige dress. I grasped my throat, expecting for the thirst to take form but I felt nothing. As more of her blood stained her clothes my physiology did not change. I was amazed, I truly was free.
"I hate seeing you like this," I whispered to the Anna who stood beside me.

One for Sorrow

"There was nothing I could do at this point, it was over," she admitted.
    Anna buried her head into my chest as the end of her life unfolded before us. As the torch was lowered down onto the hay, and the flame grew into a blaze, I turned away.
    Anna's death was a quiet one, she didn't scream like most did, the silence spoke volumes to the town.
"Can we go see how you are?" Anna pleaded with her words, too afraid to look up in fear of seeing the truth.
    I took her in my arms and lead her away from the scene. My stomach churned as I thought of the excruciating death I had experienced, and the one Anna had just experienced.
    No words were exchanged as we headed back towards the forest. The rain hammered down on Eastmere, causing small and intricate streams to twist through the forest.
    My eyes gazed into the back of Anna's head as she led the way towards her cave, the route I was now familiar with. She ducked to avoid a low branch which she then proceeded to move it out the way for me.
    Anna's caring nature was something that hadn't escaped my mind. Anna, even though she was gone, from me for a while was always part of me. My mother had always been right, you never forget your first love, they always have a pull over your heart.
"Why did I start to have visions of our time together," I enquired as the entrance to the caves was revealed.
"I was trying to let you know I was still there," she whispered.

One for Sorrow

"You have always been there," I gave a small smile and she wrapped her arms around my neck tightly.
"I love you Adrian, more than anything else in the world," her voice was so quiet that it was almost lost to the rain.
"I love you too," I whispered.

She shot me a grin before entwining out fingers together. Things almost felt clearer when I was with Anna, like everything suddenly made sense again. Then I remembered Bridget and everything I left my friends with.
"What are we going to do about the curse?" I asked.
"What do you mean?" Anna turned to me suddenly.
"We have to help them," I demanded.
"I am not sure there is anything we can do," she frowned.

If I had a heart, I am pretty sure in that moment it would have stopped beating.
"We cannot just do nothing; if you sent me visions, surely you must be able to send Bridget or Alina, or even Alexa a sign," I pleaded.
Anna sighed, "I can try, but they may only get more feelings rather than visions, I could only do it with you because I know your energy, I do not know theirs."
"Bridget is one of the unseelie; her energy should not be hard to find?"
She shook her head gently, "The energy surrounding her is too dark for me to penetrate. I may be able to communicate with Felicity," she added thoughtfully, "let's go inside now."

We walked in silence to where my body lay. The blood from the wounds had begun to congeal, glistening a dark red in the flicker of a fallen torch's embers. I felt no sorrow for the loss of my body and old-self; I have been restored to who I really was, with my first true love.

I looked around and caught sight of Anna staring blankly at the charred corpse of her brother. She did not even seem to be phased by it; she just fixed her eyes to it.

"I made my peace with it a long time ago."

I nodded my head in understanding as we both turned to see my body.

"Do you remember much of the transformation," I heard Anna enquire.

"It was agony, that's all I remember," my words were as honest as my love for Anna.

"I am sorry I was the reason for the pain," Anna gazed into my eyes; they softened as they reached my own.

Every fibre of my being loved Anna, she could see it in my eyes, she knew my heart was hers, as hers was mine.

"It has been a long three hundred years," I admitted.

"You moved on, you had Bridget. Your friends were kind to you too, even Alexa most of the time," Anna reasoned.

"You were my first love Anna, I could never let go of you. I loved Bridget, in fact I still do and I hate that I left her in the way I did. Even though you were gone, I loved you, Bridget knew that but we shared a love too, you see?" I fumbled over my words slightly, unable to understand my own words.

"I understand, you see it a lot in the new world, loved ones dying and their partners moving on, but never quite forgetting," Anna summed my words up and I nodded my head. She always knew what I meant, even if I did not myself.

We both watched as my body stirred suddenly. A groan left my lips before I bolted up. Red eyes stared at the dark walls of the cave. My hands grasped my throat as I felt my thirst appear. My current hand touched my throat as I remembered the familiar feeling. I did not have to feel that anymore.

My former self stood up quickly, his eyes darting around as he efficiently absorbed the information around him. The ghost of our daughter danced across the walls of Anna's cave, the sweet sound of her laughter echoing. I knew only Anna and I could see her. Anna looked up to me. A smile grew onto both of our faces as the ghost of Victoria faded. Anna and I quickly followed Adrian out of the cave, his pace remained as he walked through the twisted paths of the forest.

"Do you remember what was going through your head at the time?" Anna questioned.

"No, I think it was mostly just confusion," I spoke quietly.

She did not say anything else but we continued to follow him.

As I strolled through the forest, I watched my younger self. People of the town watched him, staring at him, and whispered. I knew as the look on his face changed that it had clicked, it was over, he had lost his wife and his daughter; three hundred years later and they were finally reunited.

"Why me?" I enquired.

"Your name means dark, you were always going to fall into the darkness," Anna admitted, "I am sorry it happened the way it did."

"It does not matter. Three hundred years later you brought me back into the light," a smile tugged at my lips. I entwined my fingers with Anna as I pulled her into me, holding her close.

Adrian walked past us and into the darkness of the forest, about to start his new life.

One for Sorrow

Acknowledgements-

First of all, I would like thank my amazing family, Mum, Dad, Peter, Rebecca, my grandparents and so many more who have put up with my weird and funky writing ideas for the last eight years. The thanks of gratitude extends to my in-laws as well through supporting me through the editing process, my Aunt Sarah in particular. I have to thank my Church family as well, Isabelle, Sarah, Joe, Sue, Gareth, Charlie and Louise as you have all allowed for me to keep my creative spirits alive despite not seeing you all enough as I sometimes need to.

To Abbie, my writing partner in crime and the co-creator of Eastmere. Bouncing ideas from you is basically the only way this book and the entire series has become what it is, the two hour conversations just sat in one of our cars have been priceless. This book has become what is because of you and I thank you dearly for it. And to all my other close friends, you know who you are and I love and thank you all endlessly for the support you have given me over the last years. I have never been more thankful for the support network I have in place.

And finally, to my amazing fiancé, you have been incredibly supportive as always. Despite you not being a scholar of English, you have shown interest and offered ideas which I will always appreciate. Thank you for being there for me and keeping me as sane as I can be, you and me, forever and always.

And to my readers, thank you for taking the time to get to know the characters of the book and enjoying the story. I hope you look forward to the second book as much as I enjoyed writing it.

Social Media-

Facebook- The Curse Of Eastmere Series

Twitter- TheCurseOfEast1

Instagram- tcoes_rachela

TWO FOR JOY

COMING SOON

Printed in Great Britain
by Amazon